C000274726

AMERICAN SIDDHI

By

Curtis Mitchell

Copyright © 2014 by
Flying Key Ventures, Inc.
All rights reserved.

Permission to reproduce in any form
must be secured from the author.

This is a work of fiction. Names, characters, businesses,
places, events and incidents are either the products
of the author's imagination or used in a fictitious manner.
Any resemblance to actual persons, living or dead,
or actual events is purely coincidental.

Please direct all correspondence
and book orders to:
Flying Key Ventures
PO Box 505
Hampstead MD 21074
www.flyingkeyventures.com

Library of Congress Control Number 2014952342
ISBN 978-0-9907067-1-7
eISBN 978-0-9907067-0-0

Editing and production assistance by
Otter Bay Books, LLC
Baltimore, MD 21218-2513
www.otter-bay-books.com

Typesetting and cover graphics by
Heron and Earth Design
www.heronandearth.com

Printed in the United States of America

For those who suffer unknown,
unheard and unseen,
on behalf of others;
especially those whose suffering
has been forgotten
by those for whom they suffered.

What others say I also say.
—Lao Tzu

TABLE OF CONTENTS

PROLOGUE

Credulity, my own and the capacity for it in other people, has always been problematic for me. I have within me the same capacity to believe that others do, yet I have always been unable to believe as others do. I want to, but I just can't. In so many parts of my life it would make it so much easier if I could just give up, and believe, but I can't. Some little part of myself always holds back, hanging back in reserve, some rear guard troop of reason and sanity and fear that if I ever did allow myself to believe that I would end up believing in a lie. And this reserved part of my awareness is certain that believing in a lie is a mistake, possibly a grave mistake.

Now that I'm writing about it I'm getting some clarity on the issue. I am more afraid of making the mistake of believing in a lie than I am afraid of the isolation I am consigned to by my incredulity. I don't know why this is so, but ironically, if I were to believe, I believe it would probably have to do with having seen too much trust violated, and too many mistakes made, because something was believed when it shouldn't have been. I would believe that belief itself was a mistake.

And it isn't just my personal experience that inclines me toward reserve. I see it over and over again in the beliefs of the people around me. It is as if many people are saying: "Incredible, but true! I saw it with my own eyes!" Of course, they don't mean "incredible" which would be literally saying "I can't believe it". No, they mean rather "Amazing!" and "I do believe it"! It is as if, because they saw something for themselves, instead of simply hearing, or occasionally reading, about it, that it has more credibility. Or rather, it is more knowable as true, simply because it has been seen. And yet what they were looking at all along was some feat of illusion, prestidigitation by a stage magician or hypnotist.

The big problem for me is that the stage here is real life, and real experience of the real, and the real magician is not at all apparent. Mundane and everyday life, as experienced by everyday people, is not what it seems, although to all intents and appearances (but for one intent or appearance, often), it is exactly as it seems. Why complicate it by overlaying a belief system? The answer, I think, is because life is always handing out little clues, little mysterious clues, to a deeper truth, or a less apparent truth, back behind the curtain. And not everybody wants to look there.

Two big examples of this conflict between the mundane, everyday experience, and the hidden mysterious truth are the age old beliefs that "the world is flat" and "the sun rises and sets". Everything in our ordinary experience tells us these things are so. People believed it because it worked well enough for everyday life. They would even have claimed it to be a sane and obvious truth, "known to everyone" and anyone who considered it to be not as it appeared to be ran the risk of being considered and treated as insane.

Why did only so few contemplate those small mysterious discrepancies that led to the truth? And why was the truth of the knowable, rather than the believable, fought against so hard for so long?

I find it astoundingly beautiful that the earth is a rotating sphere and that the earth and planets revolve around the sun. And I know that I am happier knowing this than I would have been had I lived and died believing in the appearance.

So, as a human seeking happiness I am primed to notice glitches in the appearances of things. I suppose I even seek them out. I seek out the mysterious.

Have you ever met someone that you've mistaken for somebody else? Just a glance or a posture seen in shadow across a room will evoke this experience. Have you ever met somebody that you swore was somebody else until a closer examination revealed that they weren't that other person? Have you ever met someone, same hair color, same body type, same eyes, same gestures as someone you knew, but it wasn't them?

Sometimes the key to the mysterious is the difference between what is discernible upon close examination of the observable and what is believed, based on the appearance of sameness day after day.

Sometimes the key to the mysterious is the opposite formulation; when things that normally appear to be different, in this case, individual persons, actually appear to be the same.

I first met Quinn in 1977 in Memphis and it was like that. We had heard stories of each other, that is, of someone who looked like us. Being a common enough looking person I thought it was probably an easy enough mistake to make, but when we met I thought that I was basically looking at a doppelganger and wondered if the stories about meeting your doppelganger were true—that it was an omen of death. As things turned out, it may have been.

At the time we were both "river rats", as we were called. We both worked on the big river towboats that push barges, sometimes rafts of barges lashed together with steel cable, up and down the big rivers. We were both Union men too, working out of the Union Hall for whatever company needed a deckhand at the moment. We had sometimes even worked for the same companies at the same time, although on different boats.

That first meeting, in the back of a bar in downtown Memphis, lasted no more than a half hour, and I didn't see him again for thirty years. When I saw him that first time sitting in the back of that bar he was weeping. After a little while, listening to him talk, I had the funny thought that if we had been twins he would have been the one that inherited all the "crazy" genes.

He talked about the freedom of people from fate and destiny, and how a free people would act and behave, how they would live and where they would move. He said he was weeping for the beauty of it, and at the loss of it. He talked about encounters with things that shouldn't exist. I didn't stay and listen to him though. I had a bus to catch. The whole encounter was more than a little weird, literally as well as figuratively; weird being another word for one's double.

When we did meet again, we circled each other like a couple of dogs, sniffing at each other to make sure we were who we appeared to be. We got together from time to time, just hanging out, or getting something to eat, talking about the river and old times and what we were doing now.

He appeared to have aged more than me, although I never asked him how old he was. One night when we were visiting I teased him about it.

He said, "You know how people say the worth of a car is determined by how many miles it has rather than how old it is?"

I said I did, having owned mostly only old cars and trucks.

He said, "Well, it's not the number of miles that wears you down as much as the condition of the roads."

He got quiet and introspective, and I chose that moment to ask him about all that crazy stuff he had been talking about so long ago in that bar in Memphis.

He said, "Well, I'll tell you, but not just yet. I haven't told anybody in thirty years, and I don't know if I'll tell it again. So let's do this right. Get yourself a recorder, one of those new digital ones, and we'll sit down and I'll tell you the whole story."

So we did that, and a little later I got the idea to transcribe it from the recording to the page. I checked it out with him, and he gave his permission, qualifying it with the stipulation that I let him read it. I agreed. The process took a few years. I was often too busy, and it was hard work. There was a lot of replaying the recording, a sentence at a time, and then having to go back and correct typos from trying to keep up. And then there was editing. As he told the story it seemed like every other sentence started with either "And" or "So".

When I was done we got together and went over it. I broke the story up into chapters, and after each chapter we would talk, and I re-corded those sessions and transcribed them in another typeface at the end of each chapter. We decided that if someone wanted to they should be able to read the first part of every chapter in sequence as a separate story, and then come back and start over to get the comments. He read these also, except for the commentary following the last chapter.

Before that, however, we did talk about the first part of this prologue, about the significance of sameness and difference and about the difference between the everyday mundane experience, and the mysterious. This is what he had to say:

Q: *"It's one of the keys, you know. One of the keys to the Mystery, when things are different that are supposed to be the same, and when they're the same but supposed to be different. It's when things move from the mundane everyday flow of time and space to a different kind of time and space. It's one of the indicators that you may be moving from the mundane to the sacred.*

Take coincidence, for example, and synchronicity. Like when two people who look like us happen to be in the same place at the same time. Or when things happen, like you think about someone and they call you within seconds of the thought. What's the mechanism that allows that to happen and why doesn't it happen all the time?

We think it's significant, that whatever is happening has more than the usual meaning. Sometimes it is just a coincidence, but once coincidences begin to repeat themselves, or once they start to pile up at the same time there's this kind of significance threshold that we cross. Too mysterious to be ignored, and then we know that something is happening that has unusual meaning.

And this is true about people too. Lots of people never have experiences like that, experiences of reality piling up like that. They go through their whole life as an everyday person, and there's nothing mysterious about it. But there are other people that this kind of thing happens to all the time. And these are mysterious people.

Maybe they're sacred people, too. Maybe not, at least as we usually use that word. But they are mysterious and mysterious things happen to them. I know a lot of mysterious stuff has happened to me, but I don't think of myself as sacred, even though with some of the things that have happened to me it seemed clear I was caught in sacred time and space.

So for everyday people the same remains the same and the different re-

mains the same. For mysterious people the same becomes different and the different, well, that can either become more different, or more the same, but not the same difference.

For everyday people, if they happen to notice the difference, it will often frighten them, or sometimes it makes them covet whatever it is that they believe is going on with the mysterious person. This causes lots of useless suffering. Remember, we're hardwired to pay attention to difference and gloss over sameness.

And you must understand that just like there are good and bad people among everyday folks, there are good people and bad people among the mysterious also. Why that is so is also somewhat mysterious, and actually a big problem for human spirituality. Lots of times the differences between these kinds of people are the same, and if you want an indicator of what's sacred and what isn't, maybe that's a good place to start. A lot of mysterious people are under the mistaken impression that they should be served by the everyday people, and have no comprehension of the extent to which it may be the other way around.

Is the mysterious person, the person with a different ability than the everyday person, an egotist? An asshole? Do they have a Conscience? Sometimes it's hard to tell the difference, because a good mysterious person will act like an egotist or an asshole if it's appropriate to the circumstance. And it's really hard to tell if a person has a Conscience, unless you have one yourself. Just because someone is siddhi, it doesn't mean they're a good person.

That's why it's important to understand the nature of suffering. Some suffering isn't even good for feeding worms or growing corn. Lots of suffering doesn't need to happen and doesn't serve any good purpose, especially not a mysterious purpose, or rather a good mysterious purpose. Remember, most people don't have a real clue why there is evil in the world, they make up stories about it instead, and then believe the stories are true. Understanding suffering is something you can do without a Conscience, and your Conscience will need that understanding later on, if it's going to function fully.

So if you want to understand the significance of the problem, and the solution to the problem, begin with understanding the nature of suffering, especially the difference between useful and useless suffering.

One thing seems certain to me though. The suffering of the mysterious is more intense than the suffering of the everyday, which means it might be harder to be good.

Look, you're in deep water here. You think you can swim? Think you can fly?"

He smiled at me then.

I admit I was not happy at the confusion I felt. I wondered if he was deliberately playing the role of a mysterious person being an asshole. No, that's not right. He was definitely a mysterious person. He may have been playing at being an asshole.

It occurs to me that anyone reading this might be confused too. I apologize for that. I recall I read somewhere that "confusion is the dirt of learning." He said to me once that he had a proof that "Before is to After as After is to Before." I have no idea what that means.

I don't know where he is these days. I haven't heard from him, and the people living at his place moved in after he was gone, so they don't know anything about him. I knew he was thinking of moving on, looking for work. I believe I will hear from him again.

I will say that his story is mysterious and significant even if I don't understand it. As near as I can tell he lived it with an eye on beauty and to being a good man, and making suffering useful. I guess that means I found him credible. I believe his story. I believe he told me the truth.

After the conversation above we took a little break, got some coffee, and then we went on and worked on the last chapter, and I have recorded there what happened then. Those events occurred before what I am writing now. And this prologue, of course, is not where I began, but where I ended.

May, 2013.

ANTECEDENTS

(Quinn, speaking into the recorder)

As a child, perhaps six or seven, I had my first prescient dream. I dreamed I was tying my younger brother's shoes the next morning, not something I often did. And that next morning my mother, cooking something at the stove, asked me to tie them. As I did so I remembered the dream, and watched what I was doing unfold as it had in the dream, in fascination and rising excitement.

When I was done, and those moments of reality corresponding to dream memory ended as the dream faded, I ran to the kitchen, saying "Mommy, Mommy, I just did something that I dreamed I did last night!"

She turned from the stove, wooden spoon in hand. She paled but then her cheeks flushed red. Furious, and hitting me on the head repeatedly with the spoon, she drove me to the floor in the corner. I was crying, and covering my head with my arms. She was crying, too, but she let me know that "No you didn't, that didn't happen. It's impossible. It can't happen and don't you ever forget that, and never, ever, tell anyone that you did."

So deep was the terror of the Burning Times bound into the souls of the women in my clan that hundreds of years later, the second sight arising naturally in a child produced only fury and terror.

That kind of dreaming happened infrequently over the next several years. When it did, I said nothing to anyone.

As a young adolescent I had many questions, but no answers, of course. Life seemed to provide no clear sense of what I was supposed to do. I read voraciously, more than a thousand pages a week, during those years, late into the night, seeking answers.

One night I was sitting in my room, holding the question in my mind, "What shall I do?," just sitting there in contemplation, and I found myself, surprisedly, engaged in what seemed to be an imaginary conversation with some higher or wiser part of myself. It advised me to simply answer questions until I found the answers I sought. When I replied to the voice, "Ah, but sometimes you have to ask a question in order to answer a question" I felt an immediate sense of danger and the voice fell silent, with the image of a straight lipped, almost grim, mouth vanishing; and I had a fading feeling of having been the subject of disapproval.

It occurred to me that this dialogue might have been with some externally arising consciousness or entity, but I dismissed this as improbable and unscientific.

In time I became almost completely disillusioned with everything. Nothing made much sense, all of the answers to my questions seemed either absurd, or lies, and understanding life seemed possibly meaningless, at best. I could not believe in what meaning there seemed to be, nor in what others believed.

The summer of my sixteenth year was a time of assassinations and riots and war. I had work on a small farm specializing in trees that required a lot of hand care. My boss and his family went on vacation, and since I needed the work I camped out in a little valley to keep working while they were gone. I took my food and water and a bedroll and tent. I also took 5 gallons of blackberry wine, and my tools and a copy of the *Tao Te Ching*.

The previous winter I walked into a bookstore, and saw the smiling face of an old man on the cover in a rack at the back that drew me in. I reached up and the book fell forward off the shelf into my hand. Because of that mysterious fall right into my grasp I was too frightened to read it for several months.

When I retreated to the valley in the face of the modern world and finally read it, it seemed to me to be the first thing I had ever understood in my life. The experience convinced me that it might be worth living my life as an experiment to determine for myself whether or not The Way was real.

Almost immediately the experiment began to bear results. Separating my self from my self, deeply apprehending my own Nothingness gave rise to freedom from desire. Freedom from desire set me free also from many things that had bound me down in cycles of suffering and pain that served no useful purpose. And then, embodying the paradox as indicated, allowing myself desire from that place, enabled me to elevate my desire into a love for life, and for the people. I developed the power to choose what desires to keep and which to rid myself of, and for a while I even became fearless.

My life seemed to have the potential to show much promise.

In due time I left home, and travelled to The City to study. After a year there, and three years after starting the experiment, I had my first telepathic experiences and began to dream transpersonally— that is, my dreams often had nothing to do with me, and seemed to be the dreams of people I didn't know, and hadn't ever met, or even events that were happening in real time somewhere else.

I was consumed at the time with answering three questions as fundamental to making sense of the aim and importance of existence. Without that understanding I could not conceive of life as worth living.

These three questions were:

Metaphysical: What is?

Epistemological: How can it be that what is, is actually so?

Axiological: What is the significance of what is?

In The City the ingenuous and awkward youth either savvies up quickly or is tripped over on the sidewalk. After a year I was not allowed to continue my studies in The City, so I sought, and found, work on The River.

The first time I shipped out was as relief for a regular deckhand who wanted to go home and spend Christmas with his family. The whole crew, including the cook, were basically folks who didn't have anywhere better to be. The Union contract didn't pay a premium for working Holidays. You just worked if you wanted work. You sat around the Union Hall, and when your registration number was the oldest you got the job. It was good timing for me, too. I was parked below the levee wall and sleeping in the back of my panel truck, waking up to fresh snow in the morning and collecting soda bottles for deposits in order to eat. The piles of snow-covered coal in the barges headed north for the power plants looked like the humps of river dragons gliding by.

That first trip was a steep learning curve, I'll tell you. You know how it was, two six hour shifts a day, seven days a week. I worked the after watch mostly, because that way I could get a meal in after every watch and then get to rest. So that meant I worked noon to six PM every night and from midnight to six AM under the spotlights, building tow, breaking tows, checking tows, pumping out the sinkers. And man, there were a lot of sinkers on that line, especially when the ice started to build up.

I remember one time trying to save a load that was going down, being held up mostly by the rigging. There was a big split in the hull, under the water line, and the pumps couldn't keep up. We had to slip a tarp down the side of the barge, and when it got to the crack, it got sucked in like it was supposed to, so we tied it off on the cavils. But it tore so it didn't slow the water down at all. So the mate and I went down the hatch, and they dropped pumps down after us, so we couldn't have gotten out too easy if the barge cracked up. We were down there in our slickers, water pouring over us. We wrapped oakum, shredded oak, around cedar shingle and pounded it into the crack with short handle three pound hammers, working from the narrow ends toward the middle, double and even triple driving where the crack widened then going back and driving in more shingle wedges when the leaks sprung out again. Every time we'd pause, the water on our slickers would freeze so the next movement would set off an explosion of crackling like a string of firecrackers around the corner.

After a while we got it to slow enough so the pumps could start catching up. Then we got the leak down to where the pumps could handle it. The water never got higher than my waders, but I was still soaked; soaked, shivering, and blue. We took cold showers to bring our temperatures up slowly, changed our clothes and went back on watch, checking hatches in the dark, slipping on the ice, hanging on with one hand to the hatch rails, clutching flashlights in the other.

I'd never had a job where life and death could be on the line like that. You could drop a line on a timberhead and start dogging it down to provide that last little bit of brake and it could bind and break and you'd lose a leg. Or a cable could snap and you'd lose your head. Or you could go over the side, unseen, and you'd be lucky to avoid the props. And if you went over in ice, you'd be pretty much done for unless, like the deckhand in the old story, you could get your hat off and slap it to the side of the barge until it froze, then hang on. Yeah, hang on to your hat until help comes. That was a good one.

I worked all that year, staying out as long as I could, turning around on another boat as quickly as I could, saving money. In one stretch I worked 89 days straight. It was the best job I ever had. Work. Eat. Sleep. Get paid. Some years later the Union was busted out, and that pretty much ruined it. One less way in this country for a man to make a really good life by hard work.

Eventually I found my way to study at a different school.

I remained engaged in my quest to answer those questions and it was during that time that I discovered something remarkable. I was visiting a woman I loved at the time, on a warm southern winter night, and we discovered that we could hear each other say we loved each other across the room telepathically, without opening our mouths.

Then later, in our passion, we summoned, without trying, a heart breath. As our hearts opened in embrace it was as if some higher heart came into being and as our hearts rose, the pulse of it imprinted on our lips, and then, with our hearts on our mouths we summoned the heart of our love. As the heart of my mouth summoned her heart to her essence a path was established. The energy of it circulated; first within each of us, then through both of us as one, then, in joining, cross-connected into the infinite path when I placed my lips back on hers, and there we moved.

There the energy circulated, it poured pulsing through the joining of the paths. We moved there until a wind came up that first rattled, then banged on the windows. The temperature dropped. The wind brought something that made the dogs in the neighbor's yard growl and bark and then leap against their fence under our window and howl against the wind. Something was being drawn toward the sacred vortex of the infinite path.

I thought that maybe it would be a good time to stop what we were doing.

The next morning she remembered nothing but that she had heard me tell her I loved her without speaking. After that, she said, she was gone, somewhere out in the universe, she remembered light, and that was all. Yet I remembered everything, and kept silent.

And then I went away, hundreds of miles into the mountains, and didn't see her again for a long time. I resumed the life of a working student. I worked as a mechanic and driver when I wasn't in class and I forgot myself and what had happened—for who could I tell it to? And it didn't happen again with other lovers. I continued to dedicate myself to answering those three questions.

Several months later at school I was convicted by my professors of not thinking properly. I hadn't known that such a thing was possible. It certainly explained why I found that much of what other people believed was essentially incomprehensible. It also explained why so few people found it easy to understand whatever it was I might have to say.

The dialogue years later:

M: "So, did you ever answer those questions?"

Q: *"Yeah, I did."*

M: "Well?"

Q: *"Well, I feel a little silly talking about it now."*

M: "Why?"

Q: *"Well," he said, drawing out the word, "I'm not sure it's important anymore."*

M: "Recapitulating the ground work of metaphysics, epistemology and axiology isn't important?"

Q: *"Ah, you know, the answers are simple. But it took a long time to work through all the complications of the questions, reducing the questions to their most basic forms, but those forms were so laden with meaning to me that the answers I came up with were also laden with meaning; and I'm afraid I can't adequately communicate that meaning to anyone. I'm afraid I'll have to go back and recount the whole process to you so that you can understand what I mean. And I start to feel tired, particularly in my head, when I think about what that would take."*

M: "Try me. Short version."

Q: *"Uh, well, the first thing you have to understand is that the answers had to be Absolutes. That is, they couldn't be relative answers. Relative truths are subject to time. A relative truth can be true once, and then it may never be true again in the present or the future. That kind of truth is a truth that was true once, participates in truth to the degree it was true, but that's it. History is like that, morality is like that.*

But Absolute Truth is always true. And everywhere true. It doesn't change with time, it doesn't change with location. And Absolute Truths are true about everything; everything that ever was, and all that is, and all that will be. And there are only a very limited number of Absolute Truths in the universe, some of which remain unknown.

The questions had lots of relative answers, and understanding the question in an absolute form was necessary to finding an absolute answer."

He paused, looking down and to the right. I prompted him, "So?" He put one hand on top of the other and leaned forward.

Q: *"So, the answer to the question of Metaphysics, the simplest form of which is 'What?' or 'What is?' is that: Everything is in motion.*

This seems like an easy enough thing to understand. But how much do you really know about your own motion? How many motions are you subject to sitting there in that chair? The earth beneath you is rotating, there's one. It's revolving, there's two. How many others? And then there are all the internal motions—not just your heart and blood but every organ has its own motion and rhythms. There is a whole science here and you know none of it.

So think of the number of motions you are subject to. How many? And what do their paths look like? In three and four dimensions. Coils? Spirals? Think of the moon—what effects does it really have at the microscopic level? Is the microscopic level effect somehow not real, just because you can't see it, and the macroscopic view denies that it exists? And, in another category, what is the effect of motion through a field? What induces, what gets induced?

Moreover, if the Universe is expanding and the expansion is accelerating—everything moving away from everything else—what does that say about you? What do you think is happening to you also, and this planet, at this very moment? For all you know, you could be expanding, but then so, too, would be the ruler you'd try to use to measure it.

Now all these motions are relative, relative both to each other and to any point in particular. But taken together, understood together, they constitute an absolute—a truth that is true about everything.

Insofar as anything is Something it must move and have motion. Only Nothing does not move.

Remember, we don't sense the very small, or the very large, nor the very fast and the very slow. And we don't sense sameness very well, only difference. There is an entire cosmology here.

The answer to the question of Epistemology, the simplest form of which is "How?' or 'How can it be that what is, is so?' and its corollary, 'How can we know it?' is that: Everything is material, which is to say that: Everything is substantial, and has substance. Everything is material. Knowledge itself is a substance.

This is more difficult to understand. It is not 'materialism'. An electromagnetic field is a substance. Love is a substance. Gratitude is a substance. And again, consider the moon. How tall do you think you would be if there was no moon?

Anything that is Something is substance. Only Nothing is without substance.

Of course, these two, motion and substance, being true simultaneously, is why everything is vibratory and energetic.

Interestingly, the cause of this may be Nothing."

M: "What?"

Q: *"This is the argument from the perspective of causation:*
> *Nothing is ever the cause of itself—You agree? Which is to say Something is never the cause of itself.*
> *Therefore, if it is necessary that there be a first cause,*
> *And if it is necessary that the first cause be the cause of itself,*
> *Then Nothing is sufficient as the cause of Something.*

I don't know the efficient cause, which is 'how?', of course. But I know that it is a sufficient cause. And that means that it can be known.

And we can tell tales all day about the ultimate cause, which is the most important question of all, the significance of all that is."

M: "You're smiling. And I'm lost."

Q: *"Yup. I know.*

The answer to the Axiological question, the simplest form of which is 'Why?' or 'What is the significance of what is?' Which, said another way, is, 'What is the source of value and meaning in the universe?' has the strangest answer of all. The answer is that: Everything has the same shape."

M: "What?"

Q: *"Yes, see there? I told you. I told you I don't want to go through it all again."*

M: "What do you mean? Everything is the same shape—you have only to look around you and see that it isn't true. There is an infinity of different shapes."

Q: *"Yes that's true, in so far as it goes. Remember everything you see is relative."*

M: "So explain it then."

Q: *"What I mean is this: all forms are variations on the same form, which means that everything has the same form, in essence. Moreover, this form can be perceived. It can be seen in everything; you have only to learn how to see it. The first time I saw it a light went off in my head, my vision was overwhelmed by an illumination arising inside my skull, and I had to hold on to the wall to keep from falling. It was ecstatic."*

He went silent. "Well?" I said.

Q: *"Well, what?"*

M: "Aren't you going to tell me the shape?"

Q: *"Oh, hell no. And deprive you of the joy of finding it for yourself? That would be a sin, with no justification except ego. Do your work. Figure it out for yourself. Let it drive you crazy. Then it will be yours, and so too will be the joy and ecstasy.*

That would be like telling you the meaning of life just because you asked. If I gave you the answer it would become a barrier to you actually understanding and being able to fulfill and manifest it consciously. Even giving you a hint is problematic if you figure it out too fast."

M: "But how does a visible shape explain things like Beauty and Goodness?"

Q: *"The shape has both a visible and an invisible form. In order for an Absolute to exist in time it has to have a relative form also. It is the form that is the source of our sense of beauty in anything, and since the Good is the most Beautiful, it is the source of the good as well. But how you know this is relatively. When both you, the perceiver, and the object perceived approach one of the invisible perfections of this form there is a resonant harmony that causes the experience of beauty, even ecstasy, in you.*

I will tell you this: A tree and a human have the same shape."

M: "What?"

Q: *"There you go again. Yes. A tree and a human have the same shape; only where the one is the other isn't, and where the one isn't the other is."*

M: "I'm clueless. I'll think about it later. But for now I have one more question: Why was that part about the sex and the heart breath so obscure? What is the heart breath?"

Q: *"That's two questions. And I stated it that way because I was speaking to those who already know."*

1

THE NEXT QUESTION

I remember traveling across the country to St. Louis, the River Town where my Union Hall was, to work for the summer. I was in a state of profound disbelief at what had happened at college, at being told I didn't think properly. I remember the hotel room I checked into, Room 677. It was a nice corner room in the most inexpensive place downtown. It was a soldier's hotel, where the Army boarded the inductees on their last night of freedom before travelling by bus to basic training. It was sometimes a pretty rowdy place.

I remember once stopping in the hall on my way out to get something to eat, and listening to loud voices when I heard a woman cry out "Untie me now. If you don't untie me right this minute I'll tell the Sergeant in the morning." I sat across the hall on the stairs and listened to them talk until I heard them agree to untie her, and I kept listening, while they, drunkenly weeping, apologized to her, and begged her in their deeply rural accents not to tell on them. She said, "Well, all right." They offered her another beer, which I remember she accepted. And then I left, grateful that I had not had to pull a hero, had not had to bang on the door, beat those men, and untie her.

I've got to talk about this again. I worked on the River. It always seemed to me that all Rivers are connected in life and in spirit through the seas. It is as if every ocean was the body of some giant dendrite, a giant nerve cell, and that the rivers and streams are axons and they are all connected by water, a sacred water of life, and that they communicate like some huge but simple brain. What I know is that what was under my feet, throbbing and rolling below the deck, was the Mother River of my land. It carried some part of the essence, both of life and of death, of all that lived in the center of the land out into the sea. Muddy and dark, wayward, and yet faithful in that way where you know change will be constant, drifting sandbars and shifting channels, hidden snags; dark water, life turned fertile by melting, as a woman might when the hand of her lover is on her. And I loved working on the River.

The River is in the deepest part of the Spirit of the Valley, and the Spirit of the Valley never dies. Deeply feminine, the River is always moving, and the work was always moving on it, from source to delta. And this motion, this doubled motion, gave everything not just a sense of unusual power that I didn't feel on land, but a sense of freedom, and also a sense of potential meaning. Every day, every watch I stood, felt rich and powerful with the potential to experience life and death at any moment.

I remember once we were tied off to the bank because of a storm warning. From the stern I saw seven tornados crossing the river, six surrounding the central seventh, a constellation of power, feeding on the treetops. It seemed that even the elements, ice and heat, light and darkness, all Nature on the River, had in itself a power of meaning that I could sense, and that I could feel, but that I couldn't quite discern, It was amazing, significant, and, because I couldn't quite get the significance, ominous feeling. Death or dismemberment was always just a mis-step away; you could fall between barges, or get sucked under the propellers. I was working on the stern of the tow once and another deckhand and I had just dropped the face cable over the timberhead and the damn mate jerked the capstan and before the deckhand could let go of the cable he was pulled overboard. It was a loaded barge so I was able to get down to him hanging off the cavil and get his hand before he slipped away. We were lucky the screw was at low rep, just enough to keep us still in the current. I will never forget the ranges of feelings I saw in his face, anger, then terror, then gratitude.

Or something could snap and in an instant you'd be looking at parts of yourself on the deck. I made a lock one time and there was still wet blood on the wall.

Death and pain were in every mis-step and Life and wholeness were in every good step and you could feel the goodness of it at the end of every watch. I worked on the River. And it worked in me.

There was another deckhand on the first boat I shipped out on that summer who looked almost exactly like an old friend of mine, someone I had known a thousand miles away and three years before. He was a little wider across the cheekbones, but his hair and eyes were the exact same shade, and even his skin was similar, although they were of different races. His confirmation, as the horse breeders say, was the same. More remarkably, every gesture, accent, and inflection of his voice was identical to those of this friend I once had. This doubling, as much as it amazed me, also seemed ominous, a warning to me at the time.

I remember late one afternoon, travelling north, having just faced up to a three by five tow. I was on the bow coiling up the mooring line when a harbor boat with just one barge slipped in between us and the bank. They were landing to drop a barge, and a deckhand on the bow spotted me and jumped up and called out, "Hey! Hey! I know you. You're the son of a bitch who came by my house and screwed my wife while I was out here working!"

I yelled back as we passed each other, "Sorry man, it wasn't me" (and it hadn't been). "I ain't no donkey man!"

He was yelling "Come back, Come back you son of a bitch. I'm gonna kill you" as we faded apart into an early mist.

It seemed to me then that my earlier encounter with that other deckhand who looked like a friend was a warning to me that trouble was coming, and coming because of somebody who looked like me. Turns out this wasn't precisely so, but trouble came, and these were clues to it that helped me be prepared.

And I had another warning. I had been dreaming, during that first month on the boat, of a woman I had never seen, of a certain color of skin, hair, and eyes. I will call her A. She had been telling people what to do, and would get angry when they didn't do it. She was powerful, and could hurt them by holding up her hand and twisting it. I saw her as if I was in the room, and yet invisible, an accidental witness. It was not dreaming of what would happen, but of what was happening.

I got off that boat in a month when the regular deckhand came back. I went back south to the Union Hall to catch another boat. Chance, or maybe Fate, gave me the same room when I walked in to the Hotel, room 677, and after dealing with registration I went for a walk.

I had, in those last months before I was told I didn't think properly, finished answering those three questions. I was not satisfied I had yet enough understanding of life to know how to really apply those answers in life, so I knew I needed to ask another question of the universe.

I was stalking down the sidewalk, angry at the way I had been treated by the school and happy that I had answered those questions. Filled with the victory of it, I stopped right there and out loud asked the universe that next question, pushing up and out of me, arms raised to heaven.

The question I asked, overcoming some deep internal resistance, arising out of and building on the answers to the other three questions, was: "What is the Proper Way of Being?"

When I lowered my arms there was a bookstore to my left and I turned in and walked to the back where the good books always were and there was a book by a student of a philosopher from another continent, dead thirty years. I had read one of the philosopher's books earlier that year and I respected what I had read there greatly. I had actually discovered in that book the answer to the second question in a talk he had given fifty years before.

I was surprised to find the book by this student there. I was more surprised by what was in the book. There was a bookmark, placed there not by the store owner but by students of the student of the man. It had phone numbers from different cities all over the country printed on it. I was even more surprised, I had had no idea that there was anyone devoted to studying those ideas, let alone that there was a nationwide network of these people.

And so, taking the synchronicity of the juxtaposition of my question with encountering the bookmark as an indication of significance, and perhaps even a manifestation of The Way, I bought the book, and a couple of others for summer reading. Then I stopped at a payphone down the street and called the local number.

Someone answered, and in response to my questions they invited me to come out to their house that evening and discuss all these matters in person.

Walking the city I made a choice between cab fare to their suburban house and eating, since my cash was running low. I was hungry, in more than one way even, and full of hope, another kind of hunger, on the ride out there.

As it turned out my hope was unwarranted.

The dialogue years later:

M: "So, what did she look like?"

Q: *"Who, A? I'm not going to describe her features. And because I know you're going to ask why, I'll just tell you. If I describe her it will build an image in your mind, and I don't want to be responsible for that, because when you meet someone with those features you'll think about A and project something from the story on the person you're with. You won't be able to help yourself.*

So this way you can have whatever image you want and it won't be charged, because it will probably be wrong. I didn't describe anyone's features for that reason."

M: "Sooo, were you telling that other deckhand the truth about not visiting his wife?"

Q: *"Yup. Was it you? And, knowing your history with women, do you expect me to believe you?"*

M: "No, it wasn't me either. And I expect you to believe me. I followed the rule, too."

Q: *"The Donkey Man rule?"*

M: "Yeah. The rule where you never tell another deckhand very much about where you live or about your woman. And if you did know, you never went around his place while he was shipped out."

Q: *"Yup. Anybody ever tell you how it came to be called that?"*

M: "Nope. I thought it probably referred to how some man was hung."

Q: *"It goes all the way back to the old days when the barges were towed by mules on the river bank. If you talked about your home life to the mule drivers—the Donkey Men—you were likely to find your wife had been visited by the time you got home. That's what an old first mate told me."*

M: "OK. I guess. I never broke that rule, and you say you didn't. So, maybe one of the others did."

Q: *"Maybe. I don't know for sure."*

M: "OK. So, why that next question—the fourth one?"

Q: *"It's dialectically congruent. Being is metaphysics, Way is epistemology, Proper is Axiological. You see? It combines the elements of all three categories of questions in one question.*

You have to know that being told I didn't think properly raised a lot of questions. What the hell is proper thinking anyway? What is proper feeling? What is the proper way of living? Do you know? Do you know anybody who does? I didn't know what it is, and I don't know anybody who does, not really.

But in the end, how could you know how well you'd lived your life if you didn't have an answer to that question to guide you?"

2

ATTACKED

The idea was that this was to be the first of three meetings, after which they could decide whether or not to welcome me to the group, and I could decide whether or not to join. At these meetings they would show me some of their study materials and goals, and would answer my questions.

I was greeted at the door by a member of the group as he was haul-ing his belongings out to his car, on his way to another group house in another city. He let me in, and I was met by three people in the living room, a man B, a woman C, his wife, and another man D.

We sat down. I was on the right hand end of the sofa, B pulled up a chair at my right, C sat to my left on the sofa, and D pulled up a chair diagonally to me. I was hungry and my stomach was growling.

B and C spoke about their activities, and their rules. One of their temporary rules was that they couldn't say certain words, in this case "Oh, I, always, get" and "very" and I wasn't allowed to use them either while I was talking to them. D said nothing the entire visit. As B and C alternated talking I would ask questions, none of which they answered, either dissembling or ignoring the questions completely.

At one point C got up and went to the kitchen, returning with a glass of water. I noticed on the way that her lower legs were identical to the woman I had known in Texas, I will call that woman P. As C returned I noticed also that her hair and eyes were similar, too.

The conversation resumed, and I grew more aggravated at their refusal to answer questions. I noticed that D's body type was the same as that of another friend of mine E, whom I would visit often on the way to the Union Hall. I thought this so remarkable that I glanced at B, and realized he was sitting in the chair exactly as would another old friend of mine, F. More over, they shared hair and eye color.

These congruencies served to put me on alert; it meant something unusual was happening. While B talked, my attention was diverted by my stomach and I noticed an odd pulling sensation, focused on my solar plexus, which was coming from C to my left. It was as if she was pulling on me, on my skin, or a sensory field just in front of it, pulling, pulling harder, and trying to tear it open.

I pretended I hadn't noticed and agitatedly asked B another question which he ignored. C said the reason I was getting angry was because I was hungry. I looked down and slightly toward her, replying, "No, I'm angry because you won't answer any questions," and then I turned to look up at B.

Right then the pulling sensation felt like it was tearing me all down the front, and B said "You may have a strong magnetism but that's certainly all you have." Then B, without moving, caught my eye somehow, and I felt a strong pull from his direction. All of my awareness seemed to be pulled down into a long black tunnel, a tunnel that went on and on. I went as far down it as I could, until I realized that if I went any further I would lose consciousness.

So I pulled my awareness back into the room, tore my eyes away from B, and broke free from the power of his gaze over me. In the recoil, C stopped pulling and fell back a little to the side.

There was silence, and into that silence, in a quiet voice I asked "Why? Why did you just do that to me?" B didn't answer.

I looked around the room at D, who was sitting there with his eyes wide, and an expression of shock and fear on his face. I looked at C. She was sitting there with her hands one atop the other on her lap, looking down, her face a deep red.

I looked back at B. He was astonished, and composing his expression, resumed his smile and calmly said, "I think we've talked enough tonight. It's time for you to go."

In that moment I remember what I believe was the image of the eyes and face of A, the woman of power of whom I had been dreaming, wavering, aligned over the face of B.

I told him that I had come in a cab, and asked if I could call one. He wanted me out of the house, and offered to take me back to the city. As I followed him down the hallway to the door I glanced in the kitchen, and there was a man standing there in the dark, whose form was roughly that of A. His eyes were black pools. I thought the pupils were wide with terror.

Then I heard a moan of pain rising through the floor from the basement, and we were out the door.

We got into his car, and he told me to buckle the seat belt, because, as he said, there was an interlock and the car would stall if he took it out of 'Park' and the belt wasn't buckled.

On the ride back to the city we talked only of small things. He told me a little about their network, and wanted to know what I did for a living. I pretended nothing had happened, wanting only to get back to town and safely disappear. I had him pull over on a one way street and drop me off several blocks from the hotel.

As I opened the door he reached over and put his hand on my leg with a pulse of power and said, "You'll be fine tomorrow." I smiled hypnotically, pretending, and answered "Yes."

I walked off in the opposite direction, ducked into an alley, and skirting the street lights made my way to my room without being followed.

I remember thinking that these were people who were developing psychic power without a conscience, and, remembering the groaning sound from the basement, that they performed experiments on innocent people, that they were evil, and had to be stopped.

The dialogue years later:

M: "I don't know what to say."

Q: *"Yes."*

M: "This really happened to you?"

Q: *"Yes."*

M: "People can have this much power? How?"

Q: *"I'm not certain. Through certain kinds of meditation combined with certain exercises. The practice of Qi Gong is useful, because these kinds of manifestation always require the expenditure of energy, and there are only two ways to get that: build it up for yourself or steal it from another source. I'm not saying Qi Gong techniques are what they used, and in fact I'm pointing to it as misdirection. Do your own work."*

M: "Steal it from a person?"

Q: *"No, that's not what I mean. And yes, it can be stolen. I wouldn't suggest you try it. There are consequences. And you should also know that when those kinds of energetic work are done in a group larger things become possible."*

M: "Why did you use only letters for names?"

Q: *"Again, I don't want any associations built up around certain names. And, for reasons you well understand, my anonymity and the anonymity of all these people is to be preserved, even the bad guys."*

M: "You said A could hurt people with a twist of her hand. Did you see her do that?"

Q: "In the dreaming, yes. I never met her in person, at least as far as I know. In the dream I saw and heard her angrily yelling at someone in front of her. In those kinds of dreams not everything is clearly lit, some things appear as if you're looking through a veil. As he backed off from her she twisted her face in anger, then raised her right hand and made a twisting motion with her fingers upraised. The man in front of her cried out in pain, clutched at his stomach, and fell to one knee. She smiled and released the twist in her hand, and man was released. The circle of people around them may have had many internal reactions, but they were trying to keep their faces clear of expression."

M: "Why'd they let you go?"

Q: "I don't know. I think maybe they thought I was hooked, or hypnotized, and wouldn't be able to help not coming back. Maybe they thought I wouldn't remember, or maybe they thought I would want to be like them. Maybe they just didn't care."

3

IN FOR A FIGHT

The next day I was scheduled to ship out. I packed up, left the hotel and took a cab down to the docks.

While I was waiting for the supply boat to take me out I called my friend E from a payphone near the dock. I'd known him for several years and he had just joined the police force.

I told him what had happened the night before. I was particularly concerned about the moaning in the basement. I recall that he concurred that it would be useless to contact the police; they wouldn't do anything about it even if they believed the story, and the group would probably already have thought of the possibility anyway.

He agreed with me that they needed to be stopped, however.

It turned out that he had been interested in the development of psychic power for several years and thought himself knowledgeable in the subject. He offered to run interference, to project shielding and invisibility energy so they wouldn't be able to track me.

I asked him how he thought it could be done, how I could stop them. He said that since they were in my dreams I could be in theirs.

I recall many images of this week. The outer images were strikingly beautiful, lightning and thunder storms over the river, rainbows, sunsets and sunrises, and the physical work of building and breaking tows was good. So was the food, well made and plenty of it.

The river kept me moving, and harder to target. Because I worked the after-watch, the graveyard shift, I was awake when they slept. And I worked it; worked at attacking the imagery of their dreams. I was angry. They had to be stopped.

The inner images were nothing pretty. I was in a fight, no mistaking it. The images of all the things we can horrify ourselves with began to come up, and they became weapons in the artillery of the imagination; mine and theirs.

About a week later we dropped a tow and docked in Memphis to await orders. I went over on the dock and into the shed to use the phone to check in with E.

I got him on the phone and he said, "Who the fuck are you dealing with? Man, get the fuck out now. I was driving down the road running interference for you and it was like some giant hand grabbed a hold of the steering wheel and spun it. They flipped my car on the highway, man. My car is totaled. They broke my arm. I am out of it. Don't call me again, and get the fuck out." And he hung up.

I thought I should call my friend P and let her know what was up, in case they came after her, her physical archetype having been present also at the initial meeting with the group.

The dialogue years later:

M: "Really? You fought them psychically?"

Q: *"Well, I tried, using the only skill set I could imagine. I don't know how successful I was at doing anything more than getting their attention directed toward me, and irritating them a little. I'm pretty sure I made it difficult for them to sleep."*

M: "What did you do?"

Q: *"Really? You want to know? Beatings, nightmares, them dying in their dreams. You have to understand. I was terrified and outraged at the way they had used me for an experiment. I could only imagine what they were doing to other people, people who had less magnetism, whatever that meant. People who might have gotten sucked down that long dark tunnel. I threw my terror and my rage at them."*

M: "They must have had a lot of power, the ability to grab a steering wheel and roll a car."

Q: *"Yeah, it is. It made me suspect they were using a bigger source of power than just themselves. Of course, it could have been that instead of grabbing the steering wheel, they simply grabbed his mind and made his arm do it. But I don't think so."*

4

THE WHIRLWIND OF THREAD

I called P. She was with my friend F. I remember thinking "Good, she's got some protection then."

I told her briefly what had happened, and that I thought she had to be careful. She seemed unconcerned, I thought. "Good then." And as a closing question I asked her if anything had changed between us, and she said no, but some part of me knew she was lying.

I hung up the phone and sighed and suddenly a very strange sensation started in my solar plexus.

A trembling seized my middle, and I had a sudden image of A looking at me, and of her seeing a silver blue thread running from me to someone, and tracking down that thread to someone else in the dark, a woman, and cutting it close to her at a weak point. It looked like P.

And as I backed away from the phone, and looked out through the shed door, up the levee, the air started to waver, like heat rising from a highway, and then it coalesced into a vortex of energy. A clear tornado formed in the sky coming from the same direction P was in, fifteen or so feet tall, eight feet across at the top, and then it extended at the base and touched down on my solar plexus. Then the entire tornado slammed into me and disappeared inside. I remembered staggering backwards, and then doubling over. I staggered out to the dock and sat down on a crate.

The pain was overwhelming. I struggled to breathe. I was blacking out. In a panic I tried to figure out why, why was this happening to me. It occurred to me that this was some kind of killing blow, and that my heart would stop, it was hammering so hard. Then it occurred to me that I didn't know what it was, really, and that I was nobody special enough that something of this magnitude, a whirling tornado of energy, should come crashing into me.

At that moment I remembered to practice the first technique of the Way, which is to separate oneself from oneself, and remembering thereby my utter nothingness, I took refuge in that nothingness, until I could breathe again, and my heart slowed to a double beat, and my sense of the size of my solar plexus shrank down to about the width of my body.

Now I was really angry.

The dialogue years later:

M: "I don't know what to say. I had a hard time believing this the first time you told me."

Q: *"It strained my credulity, too, obviously. So I abandoned belief and confined myself to knowing it was true, and really happened. Almost losing my life to it and then the enduring pain of it were quite convincing."*

M: "How long did the pain last?"

Q: *"It was like a black hollow inside me. The hollow was spreading, sending tendrils of terror and loss and betrayal out from my solar plexus and into seams in my soul like some malevolent ivy climbing a wall and expanding the cracks wherever it rooted, splitting and crumbling the wall where it climbed. It lasted a couple weeks until the next really weird thing happened."*

M: "Oh. I remember. What do you think this whirlwind was?"

Q: "I think it was an energetic thread that got formed that winter night with P, when the energy moved and circulated between us, and the wind came up and the dogs howled and threw themselves against the fence. It had been there all those months unknown to either of us. A thread like that would be visible to someone who can see. And once it can be seen, it can be cut.

Time and distance make those kinds of threads weaker, and they need to be recharged and refreshed from time to time anyway, apparently. It was made weaker still because P had become lovers with F which I didn't know. So when I asked her if things had changed and she said no, she was lying. And that lie made the thread easier to break.

I was tempted to be really angry with her about it, and I had to work hard on myself for a couple days to not hold it against her, but then I realized that she didn't really know anything about what was happening, nor did she understand what had happened that long ago night. Her ignorance made her an innocent in a way, and her lie was a normal everyday lie, and didn't come from the Mystery at all.

In the realm of the Mystery, this was all on me and my ignorance. And, of course, on A for cutting it, and my enemies.

If I had known better I wouldn't have let the thread form in the first place."

M: "What mystery? You keep talking about a Mystery and I don't know what you mean. Every time you use the word it irks me. What are you talking about?"

Q: "I'm talking about this one:

> *The Way that can be spoken of*
> *Is not the constant Way;*

The name that can be named
Is not the constant name.
The nameless was the beginning of heaven and earth;
The named was the mother of the myriad creatures.
Hence always rid yourself of desires in order to observe its secrets;
But always allow yourself desires
in order to observe its manifestations.
These two are the same
But diverge in name as they issue forth.
Being the same they are called Mysteries,
Mystery upon Mystery—
The gateway of manifold secrets.*

I'm talking about that Mystery, the Mystery of the Great Way of Virtue,
as it was described in the Tao Te Ching. And it is this paradox of both
allowing yourself desires and ridding yourself of desires that must be managed if you are to understand the Mystery. It is in the ridding of desire
that you come to understand your own Nothingness, the Nothingness that
saved me. And by allowing yourself desire you will come to understand
the Somethingness that you are, and what you can become."

M: "Oh. I find it only a little less irritating now that I know. I still
don't understand."

Q: "It takes a little study. At least you didn't laugh out loud."

---

* *Lao Tzu Tao Te Ching,* translated by D.C. Lau, Penguin Classics edition, 1963

5

THE TRIP TO NEW EGYPT

For the next week everything within me was madness. I was over-whelmed. I was in continuous pain. And I felt like I was constantly under attack, constantly being hammered on, like blows striking me from all sides. But I stayed in the fight.

I was speaking to the World a lot, but it wasn't speaking back to me except in images of madness. I was dreaming murder. I started dreaming the dreams of dozens and their suffering. When I would lay down exhausted from the pain, I would see multiple images simultaneously, and when I dreamed I would dream multiple dreams at the same time, too, dreams of the past, the present, and the future, all the while with the dreams continuing on. When I paid attention to any one dream, and then I would return to any other, those dreams had advanced.

Sometimes in a dream I would fall asleep and dream within that dream, waking to it again while still asleep, drawing an imaginary breath like an imaginary drowning man, then getting pulled out into the next dream.

The voices of the people in the dreams formed a background whisper that I could hear in the next dream, like conversation heard through a hotel wall, and even though I wasn't paying full attention, their bloody suffering and terror would pound on my soul, like a headboard in the next room against the wall, and I would wake exhausted for every watch. And I could feel the dreams continuing on, even while awake.

We got our shipping orders. We were to build a small tow, just a couple of barges, and take them upstream to a place near Cairo, and trade it off with a barge coming down on the Ohio, one of the Daughter Rivers.

On this trip upriver there was a book that came into my hands. Some other deckhand had left it on the boat. It purported to be a translation from the Aztec about the last days of the city of Atlantis. Now, umm, I don't take these kinds of things seriously, these kinds of books, but what was intriguing was, as I read through the book, the descriptions of the characters matched the physical archetypes of all the people who had been players in my story so far, including myself.

There was a High Priestess who had gotten out of control. She had accumulated secrets of power that were the deepest kept secrets of the Priesthood, and was discovering new secrets of power by manipulating the secrets she had acquired. And she had developed a letch; I guess you could say, an obsession, for one of the Priests. This Priest was married at the time and had children.

The Priests decided that the best way they could get control over her was to put that Priest's wife and children into a deep sleep and pass out the story that they had died but the priests would protect their bodies in secret while they were sleeping. And that would free him up to go and be with her.

And she, using the knowledge gained by the secrets, and using him, rose in power and became Empress and he went along with her. He didn't become Emperor but remained as her Consort.

Even as close as he was to her he couldn't stop her from doing what she was doing in order to gain power for herself. She was using this power to manipulate the fabric of time and space, bending reality to her will, and destroying the balance of nature in the land for miles around. Seeing the impending disaster caused by her manipulation, the Priests prepared boats and got the Priest-Consort's wife and children on board. As the city was being destroyed the Consort managed to get on the boat. While some of the Priests remained behind to cover the escape, most of the rest of the Priests and their families got away safe.

It was assumed by all that the Empress died when the city went down and the book ended with some more of the details from the survivors' lives written by the Priest-Consort, nominally the author, acting as the scribe for the whole story.

Anyway, as I was reading this story the images of these characters constructed themselves in my brain. They overlaid other things and other people and other circles I had known in my life, even some of my family members. I also began to see images of the characters from some of the other great stories where those peoples' physical archetypes had certain elements in common with archetypes and elements in other characters in other stories. These stories entered my dreams, too, and I began to see that they were somehow all connected and the mistakes that were made in one place got passed energetically to the next people that happened to resemble them, so that these corrupt and dysfunctional power dynamics, these archetypal patterns, kept repeating themselves, and then new mistakes would be added to them, compounding the impact as their lives unfolded through time.

I, umm, don't want to mention what some of those other stories were. I don't, I don't want to lay claim to them because it seems too much. It seems too big. But what I realized was that what was happening was something that was much bigger than me, and I was caught in a net of fates and destinies like some fish in a school of other fish who all looked alike, mixed up with other different schools of fish, each school having its own lookalikes, being drawn through the ocean of the sky, not to be pulled toward shore, but to be held trapped, forever circling.

That became even more apparent one evening when we were coming up to Cairo. There was a news report on the local TV channel of a giant black shadow in the shape of a bird that was at least 15 feet across. It had come down in a park in this little town by the river. It had attacked and tried to carry off a child but a deputy sheriff who was on patrol in the park at the time saw it. He came running up to it and beat on it with his billy club. It dropped the child and flew off, but the arm he struck the shadow with had gone completely numb. He was in the hospital and the doctors didn't know if he would recover. This was on the local TV broadcast news. Can you believe it?

The dialogue years later:

M: "Atlantis? Giant black birds?"

Q: *"Yup. Mythological stuff. Legendary stuff. The local native people had stories about that bird."*

M: "Crazy!"

Q: *"Well, that's one explanation. Another is to remember that many of these old stories and myths have at their origin a true story.*

For me the point was that if legends were coming alive then something big was happening. And that I was caught up in it. It was another warning. I remember feeling afraid all the time, and feeling an impending sense of doom.

But what I was beginning to think about was that I might have a chance to change how some of the stories that were always repeating themselves affect the people who get trapped acting them out as characters. And maybe I could even change some outcomes.

If I could change an outcome, even by changing one little behavior, then people wouldn't be so locked into the doom of repeating the past.

You know, almost a year after finding that book, when I was on the run, I ran across this psychic guy who was a wild mountain man, living up in the mountains all by himself. He used to go to the bars and talk to the ghosts that were haunting the drunks. He was a pretty wild person. He told me how he learned how to see auras and stuff so I told him some of my stuff and asked him about details of the story in this book because he had mentioned Atlantis while he was sitting there in the bar talking to me. He said 'Oh yeah! She escaped. She surrounded herself in a bubble of air and escaped.' And as he said this I saw her, under the water, surrounded by a capsule of air, and she was sobbing."

M: "Wait, what about this guy, this wild man, as you called him. Where'd he come from? And how'd he learn to see auras?"

Q: *"Well, he was just some guy. Like I said, I was on the run, and moving from place to place. Sometimes I just wanted to stop, you know, stop in somewhere and have a beer, see what a place felt like. When I walked in and he saw me he said 'What are you doing here?' which is the kind of thing that would happen to me a lot in those days. I'd show up somewhere and somebody who had some kind of sensitive ability would look at me and say something like that.*

I've no clue what they were seeing, really, or feeling, or why they would say it. Sometimes they wouldn't know either. But this guy was talkative. And I certainly noticed him, because he looked way out of place; long wild hair, older, worn out clothes. He said it was a part of his job to go into bars and talk to the ghosts and spirits that were haunting the drunks and pushing them to do bad things. He said he had a way to make them leave the people alone.

When we were talking about Atlantis he said something else very interesting. He described the High Priestess in the story, and his description matched the description in the book. You should know that this description matched A's physical description.

He told me big chunks of his life story; like how ever since he'd been a little boy he'd wanted to be able to do the kind of things Edgar Cayce could do. Since he couldn't figure out a way to safely give himself a head injury he would do things like sit in mountain streams for hours and pray until he could barely move and drag himself out. He said that was how he learned to see auras, and ghosts and things. He said he could teach me how. But I couldn't stick around, I couldn't let them catch up with me. I took his phone number but I never got back his way.

If he's still alive he'd be a very old man."

6

THE SONG THE STARS SING

So that night I was exhausted and when it was time for me to bunk down I was in incredible pain everywhere. Everything ached and hurt. I was overwhelmed, I was weak, I was exhausted, my mind was... I don't have any words for how it was. But I went to sleep. I usually woke up a few minutes before the deckhand from the other watch came around and knocked on the door. I didn't like being surprised by the knock on the door, and I had trained myself to be up and dressed without an alarm clock.

I remember that I was dreaming, and I was dreaming of a conversation with a particular, oh, kind of a guru that I'd read about in those days, and, uh, suddenly becoming aware of my body as I was waking up while still in the dream I said it was time to go because I had to wake up. And as I was waking up I suddenly smelled foul air and felt something strange in the bed.

I realized that in my sleep I had soiled myself, or at least I thought I had, because I put out my hand and there was a huge mound of feces between my legs. Then I opened my eyes and suddenly the room smelled powerfully and overwhelmingly like shit. It smelled like the room was filled with shit. I looked around, and there was shit splattered on the walls, and piles of shit on the floor, and over in the corner of my bunk room was a little hunched over black demonic form, about as big as a dog.

And in the despair of realizing that in just a couple minutes the deckhand from the other watch was going to be coming through the door and that there was no way that I was going to get this cleaned up, what was I going to do? I think I may have died.

Then suddenly I found myself flying through space towards these two stars that were close to each other and as I got close to these two stars I saw a form suspended in space, a golden haired form in some kind of dark clothing, and I came up close to this form from behind and I kind of snuck into it, merged with it from behind, and I felt a sense of surprise from the being, and in that moment I could hear the song that the stars were singing to each other, hearing them through the ears of this being.

Then I heard the deckhand knock and he opened the door.

I was slammed back into my body. I partway sat up and turned my head and saw the deck hand opening the door. His eyes grew wide with terror as he looked around the room and his jaw dropped Then suddenly I was in his head looking through his eyes. I saw a golden whirlwind forming and coming through the ceiling. Then, back in my own head, I looked up and saw it. It slammed into the top of my head and as it slammed into the top of my head all of the shit that was on the sheets and on the walls and everywhere just disappeared, whoosh, completely gone away. The demon was driven from the room.

And the deckhand said something like "Holy Shit!", slammed the door and ran down the hall.

(There was a long pause on the recording.)

It's hard to tell it all, easy enough to remember it, but hard to say.

(The recorder clicks off.)

The dialogue years later:

M: "Good grief. Demons? Shit everywhere? Really?"

Q: *"Yeah I know. I didn't think there was any such thing as demons."*

M: "I still don't."

Q: *"That's OK. I can see no reason to wish such knowledge on you."*

M: "Merging with a being in space, and then getting slammed with a golden whirlwind. What do you think that's about?"

Q: *"That's complicated, and I'll talk about it later."*

M: "What about the song? Do you still remember it?"

Q: *"Oh yes, clearly. One note, all vowels. I expect that stars don't have teeth or tongues or lips for consonants. I've been able to fit words to it though, in different languages. All I heard were six sounds, I wasn't there very long."*

M: "Will you sing it for me?"

Q: *"Sure."*

And he did. As the last sound faded it seemed to echo, and my heartbeat locked into the echo's pulse.

7

THE SOULS OF THE DEAD

Ok. I can pick it up again. Those next couple of weeks were pretty amazing, umm.

Yeah, well, that night when I went down to work, the deckhands, well, the one deckhand who woke me up had obviously told the other one the story. They were both sitting there, staring at me or rolling their eyes away and gripping their chair arms all tense and twitchy and stuff like that, as if they were dreading anything I might do or say. Or that if I said anything at all they would jump up and run away. I simply smiled at them, nodded, and went over to the galley to grab a cup of coffee.

They had traded the barges on their watch, and we had turned, so after relieving them and checking the tow, I had the whole night to ride and guide, as we called it, heading back down river. Good thing, too, because I wasn't good for much.

When I had gotten out of the bunk…I remember, when I rolled out of the bunk I had to hold onto the bunk to keep from falling. I was so overwhelmed with ecstasy I could hardly catch my breath. I was saying things like whoa, shoo, whoa, and panting, trying to slow my breathing down.

The only thought I could form was "Oh my God what is this?" I was dizzy with ecstasy. It was all I could do to hang onto the side of the bed and keep my legs from buckling. Getting dressed was really slow and hard to do. I had to sit down a lot. It seemed like everything I saw was through a golden haze.

I remember feeling really shy when I went down to the main deck, down to the crew lounge to go on watch. Those are some of the things I remember.

Like I said, the next couple of weeks were pretty amazing. We were tied off in Greeneville, doing maintenance, working up lines, replacing cables and such, waiting for orders. Those two deckhands had gotten off and two new deckhands got on, which was good, you know. They never stopped being scared, and I never talked to either of them again.

And, umm, the, uh…I remember in the first few days afterwards, umm, this energy was surging through me and it was pulsing through me in waves. It was roaring through me. It had come with the golden whirlwind. It was like I was a bell that had been rung and I just couldn't stop ringing.

A couple days later I remember a pain in my lower back and this ringing and pulsing energy was just jamming against this spot in my back that felt like a dam. Then one day the dam released and this spiral of the energy rose up my spine and dissipated at the base of my skull. It was like some door got blown open inside me. Then that energy, that pulsing, resonating energy, would circulate inside me, and sometimes outside of me, or pool in one place for a moment, then rush on and pool somewhere else.

I had thought I was dreaming broadly before but after that I was dreaming things all over the world; dreaming things that had happened in the remote past, dreaming things that were going to happen in the future. I was seeing these things while I was working as well; that part of my brain just never shut off and it was this constant flow of information and, and, arguments from me with what I was seeing because what was happening then was this:

There were these two small pools of energy concentration on the sides of my head, at the temples, that, that, well, they extended out to the side about to my shoulders, but a little higher than the top of my head, like the curved speaking horns of the deaf from earlier days. These had opened up and suddenly I was engaged in dialogue with voices that arose outside of me.

Sometimes it was just a single voice but if I listened closely other times it seemed I could hear what might have been thousands of whispering voices going into the making of that one voice. Other times it was many distinct voices.

And I would argue with them. They'd want me to do this or pray that and it was all I could do sometimes to make sure that I never identified with any of them, keeping only my own voice my own, and not letting the visuals or the pressure of the voices overwhelm me and paralyze me. Needless to say, sleep was possible only when I was exhausted, and even then I would dream dozens and dozens of dreams every night.

So it was crazy, all crazy inside me and here I was trying to work. At one point we got orders to go down to Baton Rouge to build a tow and then go on down and dock in New Orleans to wait for another barge for a special delivery.

I've got to tell you that those days in Baton Rouge building that tow were the hottest time I've ever worked outside. You had to carry water everywhere, because if you didn't you'd stop sweating, and the minute you stopped sweating you were done for, heat stroke wise. If you passed out and fell down the deck was so hot it would burn you. I had to wear two pairs of gloves, one of them welder's gloves just to touch the tools, or put a hand against a bulkhead for support. I carried a couple quarts around everywhere, one for drinking, one for pouring over my head. Evaporative cooling was the only way to go.

Normally we didn't put a loaded barge near the middle of empties because of the strain on the rigging, but because of the drop-off schedule we had to this time. I remember being down in the well on the bow of the loaded barge, finishing off the rigging, surrounded by the high riding empties, and it was so hot the soles of my boots got soft and I started to slip down the slope of the bow deck. It was too hot, and too far, to use the bulkhead for support even with the gloves, and in order to get a good grip on the cheater bar for the ratchet handle I had to hook one ankle over the barrel of the ratchet to keep from sliding down the deck. Getting out I had to climb up on a timberhead and hop up to the empty deck without touching the sides.

So we tied off the tow and went down to New Orleans. When we got there I had the afternoon off while we were waiting for the barge to be delivered so I went down to Bourbon Street just to see it. I called a cab and rode down there, got out and walked up and down the street a couple times. I decided to go into this little fortune teller's shop. I was hoping that maybe I could get some sort of random outside confirmation about all the craziness that was going on inside me.

I went up to the counter and there was a man standing there behind the counter with archetypes mostly like A, but with a little B mixed in. As I was standing there talking to him about getting a card reading this woman came in all wild hair and crazy with archetypes like P and demanded that I let her read my cards. They started arguing.

He said, "Get out! You know you're not allowed to read in here anymore."

She looked at the guy behind the counter and said, "Let me have him. You know he's mine. You know I'm supposed to read for him. You know it. Let me do this."

She looked at me and said, "Please Mister, I'm the one who's supposed to read for you."

I looked at her and looked at him, back and forth. I said to him, "I don't know what to do here."

He said, "You have to choose."

I said, "Okay it's your place. I'll go with you." to the guy behind the counter.

He said, "All right, you heard him. You get out of here now."

She turned, hair tossing, angry, and said, "Fuck you, then." and weeping into her hands she ran out the door.

So we went off to this little booth with a table and chairs on either side of it. He said, "You made the right decision. She's not allowed to work here anymore."

I said, "Why?"

And he said, "Well, you can see why, can't you? She's crazy, and she tells the customers stuff about their lives she shouldn't."

So he laid out the cards on the table, looked at the cards and rolled his eyes back in his head. His head went back and he started trembling and shaking. His eyes snapped open, his head came forward and he looked at the cards again. Suddenly he swept them all off the table onto the floor.

He sat there shaking. He looked at me and he said, "Who are you?"

I said, "I don't know. There's a lot going on with me right now and I just came in here to find out anything I could about what's going on.

He said, "You don't know what's going on?"

I said, "No, I was hoping you could help."

And he laid out a new spread, a different spread. Just for a moment he rolled his eyes up but he kept his head forward. He said, "I'm sorry but I can't tell you anything. All I can tell you is that the good news is that you're alive and that help will come, you will have help, and that's all I can say. Now you have to leave, too."

So I left, looking around for the woman reader. I didn't see her so I walked down the street. I was kind of confused. I knew the reading had been a sign that confirmed that something was in fact going on but it didn't tell me anything about what. I let a hawker out on the sidewalk steer me into a club with girls dancing on stage. I figured what the hell, it was cool and dark in there. I was thirsty and I needed to look at something pretty.

After a turn on stage a pretty girl came around to sit with me, looking for tips. She said, "You don't look like the kind of guy we get in here most of the time. What do you do for a living?" I told her and she seemed fascinated.

She told me a little bit about herself, how she was going to school with the money she was making and what she wanted to do. I told her some about what I wanted to do and she said to me, "You seem like a pretty nice guy to me. If you want to come back we can go out. I get off work at two."

I said, "Ahh, I'd love to darling, but I've got to be back on board the boat before midnight."

And I left, feeling better, thinking I wasn't crazy and I must not be too bad off if a pretty girl was still willing to go out with me.

I got back to the boat in time to stand my watch and the barge was delivered. We powered back up to Baton Rouge to cut it into the tow. That afternoon we wired in the remote controlled pilot boat on the bow, and shoved off upstream back to Memphis to drop off the barges and then dropped down to Greeneville to wait for orders again.

And the voice, or rather the voices, came crowding around again. One set of voices was like the chorus from some old Greek tragedy, an Ancient Chorus. And it would comment on things that I would think or say even when I wasn't talking to them. (Sighing) And I became more and more clear about exactly what was at stake, about what was involved in this and about how many stories, how many stories of power, and how many legends of old had a hand in shaping what was happening, and what was about to unfold. It seemed to me that the end of the world was at hand.

I asked The Chorus what was happening and the voices came back with the words "Opening the Seal. The Seal is opening." I remembered that there was something about Seals in the Book of Revelation. I had been seeing in the sky, well, it was filled with little spirals, just little spirals of energy. They looked just like dark lines in the clear sky and there were thousands of them and I would, I would focus on one and I would get an image or an emotion. I could hear a noise from them but I couldn't make out the words. Most of them were angry and wanted vengeance, and they wanted the world to end because they felt betrayed.

I saw a vision of those little spirals attacking my friends; the spirals were trying to get in their heads and put thoughts in their heads and they were trying to do this to other people that I knew. There was this huge pressure that came from them, a pressure to make the story go a particular way, a pressure to end the world. That's what it felt like.

And I refused.

The dialogue years later:

M: "Those 'speaking tubes', seriously. What are you talking about?"

Q: "Yeah, well, I, what I think now is that they were minor chakras that can become activated and have a higher function. Remember, I didn't understand all this stuff while it was happening. I didn't know any esoteric anatomy; I didn't know what chakras were. These were all things that I found out in subsequent years, when I was trying to figure out what had happened to me. I found a clue in legend, where they were apparently called the Horns of Moses.

The Horns of Moses are a legendary thing that you can sometimes see in paintings of Moses. They're usually depicted as two columns, or cylinders of light that originate in his temples and extend outward a couple feet into the air. They would become visible to the people, surrounded in a halo of golden light, supposedly when he was speaking and listening to God.

That's not exactly what I felt, though. What I felt was more like those spiral curved ear tubes that old people used to hold up to their ears to hear better. One day, a few days after the Chorus showed up I noticed them, but they'd been there, open and working, for several days already."

M: "And the pulsing energy? What was that? And especially what was the dam in your back about?"

Q: "Look, you need to understand that I didn't know what any of this stuff was while it was happening to me. It was years later, especially when I was living in the wilderness, coming into town occasionally and buying books, that I was able to find any terms or historical precedent about these things.

The pulsing energy was like what I had experienced before, that night with P, but never after that until this time. I'm still trying to figure out some things about it. It tends to pool in the chakras, and it tends to circulate, and change frequencies. It resonates with different possibilities and experiences in different ways and locations. And it is transmissible too. I might say more about it later.

The sensation of the dam bursting corresponds to what I've read about, what is called in India 'the release of the Kundalini serpent'. The increase in sensation and perception I experienced that followed on its release are pretty classical, in those traditions. It took many years to get all that under some kind of control.

Everything hurt in me. My whole body hurt all the time; I felt like a balloon with too much air in it. Or like a pipe with too much water flowing through it, about to burst.

I had to work and stay in the world and still deal with all this stuff. I felt like I couldn't trust anything happening inside me, there was no safe place within me, except my sense of my own nothingness; that I was nobody important, that there was no good reason this was happening to me. Work, real physical work outside in the southern summer heat was the only thing I could trust."

M: "I'm sorry, friend. I'm so sorry it was like that for you."

Q; "At least I had the work, a focus I could go into wordlessly. Without it,

I don't know what would have happened."

M: "There's one more thing I need to ask you about, and it's about that Book of Revelations stuff."

Q: "Check out the Book of Revelation, Book 6, Verses 9 and 10. I didn't know the passage at the time. The only words from the Chorus were "It is the opening of the seal". Revelation wasn't real big growing up and it had been years since I'd given it even a passing thought. I'd dismissed the whole thing as a fairy tale, even.

That passage is about the opening of the Fifth Seal, and the souls of those who had died for the word of God, crying out that their blood be avenged on those that dwell on earth. They were angry that the vengeance had taken so long. Since some of them had died believing that the Return of the Lord was imminent when they died, they felt they had been betrayed as well. I read somewhere since then that in the early days the Return was expected within the lifetimes of those who had known Jesus. And then there was the Millennium. And there have been several dates for the Apocalypse since then. Even in our lifetime. Again, remember that I didn't know any of this at the time, and had only the vaguest recollection of any of it from the stories of my childhood. I remembered at the time only that seals were mentioned.

For me, what was important was that I was seeing and feeling these little spirals, and their thoughts and feelings when I allowed myself to perceive them, were spirals of anger and the desire for vengeance and the despair of dying betrayed. And sometimes I would see images from how they died, and feel their feelings while it happened. And if I looked too long or felt too long, I would start to feel like them.

But I had to remain my own self, I had to remain what I was."

8

THE DEAL

And so it wasn't long before I became unable to trust anything that happened inside me because I came to suspect I was also getting directions and commands from what I believed was the Being who had been watching the stars. This one voice seemed to be coming from closer in, and I would feel things inside me when it spoke. It was as if I could almost see it. So I had to hold myself down to just the barest thing that I could be above nothingness and still be in control of my body and work; keeping my awareness inviolate, and maintaining the ability to control my limbs.

This was in addition to ignoring the visuals, you know, the forms and shadows that cut across the periphery, and haloes around everything, the audibles from the Chorus, and the terrifying and despairing images from the dreams. My dreams would continue all day, too, while I would be working. I only had to close my eyes, and I'd see them.

I remember we were tied off at Greeneville still, and we were waiting for orders there. I remember chipping the paint off the bulkheads and decks with a pneumatic chipper, so they could be repainted, all through the long hot afternoons. The whole time I was out in the sun I'd be engaged in dialogue, and it would either be with the

Chorus, or it would be with other things that were more internal than that, parts of myself, or that voice. My mind was filled with visions of possibilities and things that could be done.

Somewhere in this time I remember the Chorus asked me what I wanted and I told them I wanted to live a long time, and have a great many children and become a healer. I felt some wave of judgment coming from them, a kind of thoughtfulness neither negative nor positive but they didn't say anything in response.

After all these days working and living this way I thought I came upon an idea that might just save the situation and make everything work out, but I had to hide the idea in my mind just before verbalizing it internally.

Finally after my watch one day I went out for a walk along the levee in the evening. I was walking along the lower levee and there was some kind of carnival up above on the bluff. I could hear the music from the carousel, and people talking and laughing. I just started walking toward the music (long pause) and I told Them, Those Spirals Above, I'd make a deal with Them. I said, "I tell you what. I'll make a deal with you. Your freedom in exchange for Mankind's."

And they actually stopped agitating and jumping and spinning around up there. I had their attention, and I could feel something thinking.

Made confident then by that response, I looked up and said "Yeah, that's it. The price of your freedom is mankind's."

And then the Chorus said, "And the price of mankind's freedom is yours."

I said, "Fine. So be it."

And the Chorus echoed, "So be it. So be it. So be it."

And that sky full of angry and vengeful spirals disappeared. I could hear faint zips, and whooshes and pops. Some fled in certain directions before they disappeared, some just vanished in place. In almost an instant the sky was just sky again.

I turned and walked back up the levee toward the boat, then my guts churned and heaved so badly I had to squat down in the high grass with the sumac waving over my head and take a dump right there, in the tall weeds there on the levee with the sun setting across the river. When I was finished I just walked away.

Now we'd been tied up there for some days, we hadn't been moving, when that happened and, umm, we got our orders and we shipped out again. I need to say that on the river during this time, for a couple weeks before and a couple weeks after, I remember that it seemed like people were getting closer to the boat, and to me. It started with one man and then later with people coming to the edge of the levee, and looking down at us, the same group coming back at different times, as if see if we were still there.

Later, when we were moving, I would see people driving along the river banks as we passed, you know, pacing the boat. I saw a car one time, one that was identical to the car I was in when I left the Group's house. There was a time when I saw people lined up on the river banks getting out of their cars and staring at the boat when we were going by.

I remember one time passing someone who was driving like hell, driving like a bat out of hell, all up this river road. I could see the driver yelling at me through his open window, and the feelings coming from him were rage and the urge to terrify. Then this thunderstorm came down and covered the boat. We went upstream and dropped off a barge at the tow in the rain. Then we turned and headed downstream and that truck turned around to follow us again to where more barges were tied off. Then the storm closed in so thick I couldn't see the bank. We picked up a barge moored to a different piling than before and turned and headed back upstream to the tow. The thunderstorm turned and followed the boat. The rain stayed with us, a thick impenetrable curtain.

And I remember that whenever it rained the images would be fewer and the volume of the voices would get less. It was as if the Rain and the River were a protection that were working together to keep me safe. I have no doubt that the River saved my life.

The dialogue years later:

M: "What were you thinking? I mean, what were you thinking, what was your internal dialogue, such that it led you to making a deal like that?"

Q: *"Like I said in the story, there was a tremendous pressure coming from them, coming from all around it seemed. It felt like there was a force that was acting on me, pushing on me, trying to compel me to act in one way or another. The Spirals would crowd around, close in, and the Chorus was persistent and adamant.*

Judging by what was being said to me, since the contact with the Golden Whirlwind, I had come into a position where I could influence events—since I could see them, the angry dead, and feel them, I could do something about them. If nothing was done then events would proceed in the direction their momentum was taking them.

Since doing nothing seemed out of the question, I thought about all kinds of possibilities about what might be done, following out the consequences of any choice I might make as best I was able. Every choice seemed to lead to more complications, and more suffering. A lot of the choices involved some kind of self-elevation that seemed ridiculously egocentric to me, and unwarranted, given my basic nothingness. Every path, every choice I could conceive of seemed to end in tragedy. Everything I could think of, even using what felt like prescient dreaming day and night, showed me that in the end the victory would go to forces that weren't in the best interests of the people. I could find no path to a bright and beautiful future.

In the end, I tried to imagine what the best person I could imagine would do, and then I would try to do that."

M: "But why freedom?"

Q: *"Were you not listening? What else was there? Control? Power? Don't be a fool."*

M: "Ok, ok. I get it. I get it. But why deal with them?"

Q: *"Well, the more time I spent thinking about and feeling the angry dead, the more I began to understand something about them. They weren't filled with love and grace, they were souls filled with anger and a thirst for vengeance. And they couldn't be any other way—they had become what they were either right before or right after they had died.*

It was as if they were holograms, or crystallized energy forms, frozen in their feelings, and they were stuck being that, unable to be anything else until they had been avenged. They were stuck in the suffering of what they were, unable to change.

By all I could tell, whatever they were, and whatever was happening, they were a force driving things in a certain direction, they were a weight pushing events toward a certain outcome, and although I didn't know for sure what that was either, I thought it probably involved lots of suffering and destruction and the end of many good and innocent things on the earth. You know, the Apocalypse. It seemed to me that this not only wasn't the best outcome, it was a terrible outcome for all the other peoples on earth, and for the Earth herself.

So it occurred to me that freedom for those souls meant freedom for the people, and for the earth, and freedom from whatever outcome their clamoring need for vengeance portended.

After all, the whole point of a prophecy is to get people to change their ways so that what would have happened doesn't happen. Other parts of the prophecy might still come true, but this part wouldn't, and neither would anything subsequent that might depend on it.

So, freedom for them meant freedom for us.

And there was one more element in my thinking. For better or worse, I had a deep love for the people. Not just my own people, but all people. And aren't a free people more noble and more beautiful than a people enslaved to a destiny not of their own making?

And then wouldn't the dead themselves become more noble and beautiful?"

M: "So how did you suppose it would happen? The deal, I mean. How did you think it would go down?"

Q: *"I had no clue. I'm pretty sure I hadn't even thought that far ahead when I spoke it aloud. Remember, I was afraid to think about it, deliberate about it, in fully formed words internally, because that would have given it away—since I could hear 'Them' I assumed they could hear me. I'd just thought far enough to offer the deal and see what happened. But I knew that if the deal was accepted that, whatever happened, life was going to be different than it would have been otherwise, because the prophecy wouldn't come true.*

That part about the price of man's freedom being my freedom, well, all I knew was that I would have to just wait and see what it meant. Maybe it would mean my life."

9

DEATH AND REBIRTH

So I remember, I think it was two or three nights after I made that deal, not knowing how, or what, would happen next. But the immediate pressure was off. For me it was like "Okay, the price of man's freedom is mine, whatever, whatever it takes" and, uh (long pause) one night during the middle of the watch we were just riding and guiding, you know, and I was suddenly overcome with this incredible rolling wave of pulsing sensation and it would start at my feet and rise up in these waves that would just travel continuously all the way up my body with this huge squeezing pressure just wrapping me and coming up over my head like that.

I remember that during the beginning of it I had been rereading that Atlantis book. The other deckhand on my watch came in the crew lounge, sat down and looked at me. He watched what I was going through and out of the clear blue he said, "So I see you're getting your initiation into the mysteries, aren't you?"

I said, "Why did you say that? What mysteries? What do you mean?"

He said, "I don't, I don't know what I mean. I just said it. Leave me alone." Then he left me alone.

The contractions, these rolling waves of compression encircled me, and went on a long time, slowly becoming more intense.

Then suddenly a vision appeared above me while I was lying on my belly on the couch in the crew lounge. I was looking up over the arm because I couldn't stand, since the sensations were so overwhelming. Suddenly this vision appeared over me. It was a woman who had some of the characteristics of A and some of the characteristics of the other players, but her body was the color of dusk, with dark hair long and thick, and it was dark where she was.

This woman was giving birth and what was happening was that I was being born from her except I was being born feet first and the waves that I had been experiencing were contractions, her contractions. As I was born I looked back up, and as I watched, her virginity restored itself, like a flower blooming except the petals were unfolding inward. And then she died. I felt the heartbeat stop.

And the Chorus said, "She is dead. She is dead. She is dead." And I said, "May She rest in peace, may She rest in peace, may She rest in peace."

Then I had a clear sense that A may have died along with Her.

Now I don't know to this day what moved me to do this but when it was over I sat up and said "Now, I don't know what this power is but I haven't done anything to deserve it and whatever it was that needed to be done has been done now. You can have the power back." And those last words echoed twice more.

Then that power that had been with me since the encounter with the golden whirlwind suddenly and completely left me. It flowed out from my mouth, from my nose, from my ears, from my eyes. It flowed out through all of the places where it had pooled; it flowed out through my fingertips and the pores of my skin. It flowed out of me like water or the wind, like breath. And rising up in a faintly golden cloud, it disappeared.

I was left sitting there empty and hollow and quiet. Even the pulsing was gone.

And then I got scared. That, that was one of the things that had happened to me after the golden whirlwind had come; I had gotten my emotions back.

After, after the whirlwind of the thread, I had come to know terror for the first time since I had started on the Way. I had been fearless for years before that. Then after the golden whirlwind, all the emotions that I had rid myself of, and all of the feelings and things that I hadn't felt in years, they all had come back, so I was this, I was this, completely, what I was feeling. I had everything in me that you could feel and experience about those feelings at the same time.

So I got really fearful in that emptiness and hollowness after I gave the power back. I ran outside and up to the bridge deck below the pilot house and I sat there trembling and afraid because I thought I had done something wrong. And I said aloud to the night sky, "What have I done?"

As I looked up I saw a vision of all these lines, all these bright lines of forces, maybe a dozen or so, coming in from all directions, all meeting in a single point, and then one last line was coming in and as that one last line was coming in I saw myself as having reached up and grabbed the center of that intersection and just pulling it, out and down, and all the threads broke and flashed off into space.

I continued looking and the sky was exactly half bright from sunrise and half dark from the night and there were these bird shaped clouds, long wings, ranks of them, dark clouds flying out of the darkness toward the light and right before they got to the light a high wind came and dissipated all of them.

After that, I thought that what I'd done might have been a good thing.

Then the watch was over so I went inside and slept for a couple hours. I got up and went outside around 10. It was a beautiful clear day with a blue sky and the Mother River had little mists, little whirlwinds of mists all over her, dancing in and out and around each other, like I'd never seen this far into summer. And instead of the River being muddy brown, she was running blue.

It was beautiful and I felt the deal was done.

I'm going to turn this off now because there's some stuff I want to say but I'm not sure I want it recorded.

The dialogue years later:

M: "So who was she, and what did that business about her virginity mean?"

Q: *"This one was pretty mysterious to me, because it seemed to come out of nowhere. I've thought about it a lot, done lots of reading and I've thought about it a lot more over the years. In the end one of the levels of meaning ended up being what I initially thought it was, once I developed a kind of certainty, a kind of understanding about the weight of suffering on the world, and how it works its way out.*

Wherever She was it seemed it was a long time ago. She was in a room with white-washed mud walls, and it was lit by only starlight and moonlight. What I could see seemed to be obscured by a dark gray haze or smoke.

The first thing I thought was that it was some kind of ending for that High Priestess of Atlantis, or that maybe it was about A and that she had been raped or abused early in life. But the imagery seemed to have deeper meaning than that. I thought of it as some kind of restoration of a balance, like the undoing of a curse.

And that led me to thinking of all the women who had their virginity taken against their will, all the rape, all the unwanted children born from rape. And how all the pressure from all this terror and rage and grief and suffering could crystallize in the collective unconscious—the mind sphere of the earth, the collective mind, both conscious and unconscious—as I understand it now. Maybe it was just the tragedy of dying in childbirth. It was as if She was every woman. Maybe, on some level, She was all women.

What better way to restore something so out of balance than to restore the virginity itself? To return something to an original condition? And that the woman in the vision died as the virginity was being restored seemed to me to indicate that the out of balance consequences of her being violated may have been keeping her, and the energy of that crystallization, alive, and trapped in a curse of repetition, like the souls of the dead martyrs had been. It seemed like a resolution of what may have been the deepest need for vengeance; a restoration that led to a final freedom.

And then something else occurred to me, something that put the incident further into the context of the deal.

If a certain kind of person had been born to a virgin, as an exception to natural law, then what kind of person would be born to a woman who became a virgin after giving birth? What relationship might the latter have to the former?

Historically and mythologically, what story might that refer to?"

M: "Oh."

Q: *"Right. And no man who isn't a fool would want a piece of that destiny. It occurred to me later that by giving up the power that had been with me, I foreclosed on the chance for that nasty bit of prophecy to manifest, too. It would have taken a lot of power to pull it off, more than any regular guy would have. Just because one part of a prophecy isn't going to happen doesn't mean that all parts of it won't. Things shift, sometimes they come through a foot to one side or the other, but that doesn't necessarily mean the result will be any better, or any less a re-enactment, a re-enslavement to the patterns of the past.*

Sometimes though all it takes to get a better outcome is to shift something that one foot to either side. But if you can remove an element from the equation, or maybe two, or even three, then the whole thing falls apart.

I'm still trying to figure out what happened there, and what it might have meant. The images and the sensations were so archetypal that it felt shared on some level with everyone who was ever born, and the mothers that bore them. And then, too, to all the terrible morality attached to virginity and imposed on women over thousands of years.

It felt like a rectification of some terrible violation of that which is naturally so, a restoration owed to, and I hesitate to say it, to the Divine Feminine Herself. I would not have thought so at the time, as I knew nothing yet of Her Ways, but now, as I have studied I have come to realize more the extent of the field in which this story played out. And even this broader level of awareness reinforces that sense of my own nothingness; I was just some accident from the mundane world who stumbled into a war in the world of the Sacred and a psychotic usurpation of the natural order in the world of the Divine.

Why take what would be given eventually anyway? And why withhold with no hope or promise? Why take when it is not the taking that makes it one's own? Only giving and earning will make it one's own. There was never any guarantee that we could have what we want just because we want it.

So, it wasn't about me, I know. But I also know that I really don't know why it was or what it was really about. If it was a sickness in the soul of the world, I don't think even love would be the cure. Maybe growing up might be, though.

And yes, before you ask, the Mississippi really was running blue with little mist whirlwinds dancing all over it. Everything seemed clean and happy."

M: "So, why did you turn the tape recorder off?"

Q: *"Do you remember what I talked to you about?"*

M: "Yeah, but why?"

Q: *"Well, times were different then. Outing somebody could have meant their lives would be destroyed. And times are even more different than they were five years ago when I first told you.*

When I knocked on the Captain's door he told me to come in, and there was the forward watch playing some version of hide the sausage. The captain was in the bed under the blanket, smirking, and with an obvious erection. And the other two were standing on either side of the bed smiling at me. I smiled at all of them, it was obvious what they were doing. I asked the Captain to put in for a relief deckhand for me, he said he would. He said something else, I forget what exactly, probably some joke about finding some relief, but I recall saying something like 'No thanks, y'all have a good afternoon' and closed the door.

M: "So why'd you leave it out?"

Q: *"So why am I including it now?"*

M: "Yeah, that. Why are you including it now?"

Q: *"Because this is one of those areas of life that have had too much useless suffering. Because I've come to understand some things I didn't understand at the time.*

Look, there's at least this: since our remote ancestor diverged in the hominid line before chimps and bonobos diverged from each other that means that we have both chimp and bonobo behavioral paradigms in us instinctively. Probably even genetically. So whenever I look at human behavior I ask myself is that chimp behavior? Or is that bonobo behavior? In so far as behavior patterns are biologically driven, we have both paradigms in us, although it's likely some of us are more one than the other. It's been a very useful distinction."

M: "So which are you? Chimp or bonobo?"

Q: *"Knock it off, funny man. Better you should answer that question for yourself."*

10

BREAKDOWN

So it was time for me to go.

I went up to the pilot house to put in my request for a relief replacement with the captain. The entire forward watch was there and they were smiling and laughing. They started shaking my hand and pounding me on the shoulder and back like I had just done something great but they had no idea what they were doing or why. The captain told me to remind him after he came off watch. My replacement got there in a couple days.

We docked at Memphis. I stowed my sea bag up in the loft of the dock shed. I kept my knapsack and a banjo I was trying to learn how to play at the time and I took that and my knapsack up the hill to the bus station. The knapsack had all my ID in it and most of my cash. I bought a ticket for the next bus back to St. Louis and I put the knapsack in the luggage storage. Then, uh, I went to the bar next door to have a beer.

After buying the ticket I had enough money left for a couple of quarts of beer. And, for the life of me sitting here now, I can't remember why I was going back to St. Louis. I guess I had some idea about finishing it off with that group of people. And I had some business to take care of at the union hall, pay my dues or something, something like that.

(Long pause)

I remember sitting in that bar, and I was the only white man in there, except for the owner who was tending bar. I sat there in a booth in the back, sipping my beer. Sitting there at the table next to me were five or six old deaf guys, sitting there drinking and telling dirty jokes in sign language and laughing uproariously in that high strange voice deaf people sometimes have when they laugh, and slapping the table and falling off their chairs. There was something in the pathos of it that touched me and I started to cry.

And then another deck hand came in, I could tell he was a river rat by the way he was dressed. That would be you. You came back and sat down and ordered a beer. The bartender looked at me funny when he came to take your order, remember? Remember those guys sitting next to us? And I remember telling you all kinds of crazy stuff about what was going to happen, but of course never did.

After that you left and I sat there and tears just pouring out of me, just pouring down my face but I had to stop crying to go catch the bus. I finished the beer, and got up. It was time for me to go.

So I went to the bus station and it turned out I had missed the bus. The clock in the bar was the only clock in any bar I'd ever been in that was 10 minutes slow. Mostly they're 10 minutes fast, you know? So I'd missed the bus and that simply added to my woes.

And that's when I went back to the bar and bought another quart of beer with the last of the change I had in my pocket.

All the rest of my money was in the knapsack, and all my ID was in there. I was totally broke now and I was sitting there still crying because I was thinking about everything that had happened and not knowing what it all meant, really. I'm sure I was crying from that sense of emptiness inside me, too, from when I gave the power back. And I sat there weeping until I had drunk almost all of that quart of beer. Even missing the bus was part of what added to the sadness.

Suddenly there was this cop standing there, right there next to me, right at my elbow and he was about that tall, almost like E. He must've just made the minimum height requirements for getting on the force.

And, umm, he said "You have to get out."

And I said, "Okay. Why?"

And he said," The manager wants you out. Right now."

And I said," I'll be happy to just as soon as I finish this beer." I raised the glass to finish the beer and the cop knocked it out of my hand with the back of his hand, spilling the beer and shattering the glass when it hit the floor.

Then he said, "I said get out. Now!"

I remember thinking, "That was rude." I went to stand up. I put my hands on the table. I stood up real slow and as my legs came out from under the table suddenly as my head passed his and while I was still coming out from under the table his eyes got wide and he got really scared. As I was standing all the way up he grabbed me and threw me up against the wall. Then he punched me in the chest, grabbed me and turned me around and threw me up against the wall again. Then he handcuffed me.

And I said "I refuse to resist."

Then he grabbed my arms and threw me towards the door. Everybody was staring and moving out of the way. I said something like, "Guys, will you make sure that banjo gets on the next bus to St. Louis."

He said "Banjo, what banjo?" So he went back and got the banjo, came back and pushed me out the door.

When I got out the door suddenly there were two squad cars and a paddy wagon outside and there were cops out there rushing in and they grabbed me as I came stumbling out the door with my hands cuffed. Then they swung me around and slammed me face first up against the wall outside.

And I said "I refuse to resist."

Then one of them grabbed my arm while the other one grabbed my arm on the other side and stood on my foot. Then the first one pushed me, pushed me so hard that I stumbled into that other cop, and he said "What's the matter with you? Are you drunk?"

I said "No sir. It's just that this other officer over here was kind enough to step on my foot for me to keep me from falling while you pushed me into him."

Again I said "I refuse to resist." They slammed my head against the wall, and I said it yet again, "I refuse to resist."

They were pretty angry and asked me if I was a smartass. More patrol cars were coming in and another paddy wagon showed up. The first paddy wagon backed up to the curb and somebody had opened the doors. Then they just took me, swung me around and threw me into the back of the paddy wagon, my knees and shins banging on the edge of the back step there. They threw me on in face first and slammed the door.

The dialogue years later:

M: "I don't know what to say."

Q: *"Me neither. I just lost it. I couldn't keep it together anymore."*

M: "You freaked me out, you know. All that stuff about how things had changed, and what was going to happen and people suddenly showing up and moving now that they'd been freed."

Q: *"Yeah, I know. All kinds of possibilities had opened up. All those different paths were just streaming through my head and I just babbled whatever stream my mind was following."*

M: "The weeping was frightening. You just sat there, tears rolling down your face, choking on sobs so no one would hear you. Your voice sounded like it was coming from under water."

Q: *"Yup."*

M: "I got on that bus to St. Louis."

Q: *"Really?"*

M: "Yeah. If I'd have known..."

Q: *"You didn't know? I didn't tell you I was waiting for the bus?"*

M: "No, you were talking about going east and going west, but not to St. Louis."

Q: *"I remember."*

M: "I didn't think we looked that much alike. Maybe kind of a gloss of each other. But it was a shock to see you sitting there. I knew right away you were the one I'd heard about."

Q: *"Yeah I knew it too when I saw you walk in the door. That you were one of them that look like us, anyway."*

11

GRACELAND JAIL

They took me to the main city jail downtown, got me out at the end of a hallway and took me up to a booking desk with a wire grate around the window over the counter. Behind it was this room where they put people's stuff. A policeman was standing there behind the counter and he asked me my name. I tried to tell him, tell him my full name, you know, trying to spell it out, but the cop just kept pushing me and I kept saying "I refuse to resist." It's what I'd been saying out there on the sidewalk. I said it every time he pushed me and every time I said it he'd push me again.

The cop behind the desk was a Lieutenant and he asked the cop who'd arrested me, "Why'd you bring him in?"

The cop answered, "I don't know. I just felt threatened."

The Lieutenant said, "Threatened? How? Did he say anything? Do anything?"

And the cop said, "No, he just stood up."

The Lieutenant said "Well, what the hell do you want me to charge him with?"

The cop said, "Drunk and disorderly. We can hold him on that overnight." So he wrote me down for that.

There was a shift change going on and the hallway was really crowded with cops coming and going. The one holding me kept pushing me and I kept saying "I refuse to resist." And I kept trying to spell, and then say, to the Lieutenant my full name. All of a sudden this one cop who was walking down the hallway must have heard the 'uinn" as "you win".

He grabbed me and threw me backwards down the hallway. I was off-balance and backpedaling with my hands still handcuffed behind me. Then he ran towards me and launched himself through the air, grabbed the front of my shirt with his hands, landed on me with his knees on my chest and I slammed down on the floor with him screaming at me, "Of course we win. We always win."

Boy, when the back of my head slammed down on that stone floor, whew, the crack of it echoed off the walls. I saw stars and I blacked out for a second, I think. And the cop let go of me and stood up. He stood there over me with his fists clenched. I was so full of panic; I did not want to die on the floor that way. I swore I would die on my feet. When he took his eyes off me I just started scrambling, backing up, pushing myself along the floor with my feet, until I came to a wall and using it for support I pushed myself up to my feet.

I just stood there, back to the wall, staggering and swaying, looking at this cop, the hallway spinning and narrowing, trying to figure out who was going to come at me next. And I said it again, real quiet, "I refuse to resist." The one who jumped me turned and walked away. Two other cops came after a minute and took me into the elevator. On the way up to the tank they laughed and one said, "Remember all the fun we used to have in here?" The other one smiled and said, "Yeah, yeah, we used to have a lot of fun."

So we got to the next floor. They took me down the hall and threw me into the tank. There were about 10 other guys in there. There was a shitty little toilet and a sink over on the back wall. It was a summer night but it was cold in there. The reason it was cold was that they circulated chilled water under the steel bench and you had to sit or lie on it. I could hear the water gurgling in the pipes. It would suck the heat right out of you. Some of the guys had taken all the toilet paper and wrapped it around their arms and their torsos to keep from shivering in the cold.

I lay down on the bench. I remember singing all the songs I knew, still being an asshole, singing them loud, and then I fell asleep. Actually, I think I passed out from getting my head cracked on the floor. When I woke up the pain in my head was tremendous; it was terrible.

As I woke up I realized I had been crying in my sleep and my tears and snot had all run down from my face. Coming to, I realized that my head had been lying in a pool of my own tears and snot on the bench, that's how much I had wept in my sleep. And I remember saying "If help is going to come, you better come soon because I'm going down."

I was passing out, falling into some deep darkness, sinking quickly through levels of worlds it seemed. The door of the cell opened because a cop was putting a new guy in the tank. That pulled me back up to the room and I opened my eyes because I was right there by the door. Then I saw the Golden Whirlwind coming down the hall and it blew the officer out of the doorway and it blew the other guy into the cell. The Whirlwind slammed down into the top of my head again and disappeared into me. The officer jumped back from the far wall and slammed the cell door shut and ran down the hall.

When the Golden Whirlwind slammed down into the top of my head and disappeared, it completely vanished away all of the tears and all of the snot. It completely dried my soaked shirt and it sat me bolt upright. I was sitting on the bench with my legs crossed, I think maybe in a full lotus, a position I'd never been in before and have never been able to get in since. All I could see for a long time was a Golden Field. I was immersed in this Golden Field, suspended in it, floating. Pain gone, lost in ecstasy, I was vibrating and pulsing with an energy like I had been the last time it descended into me.

As the field cleared and I came back into the cell I saw the guy who had been tossed in was sitting next to me. His eyes were all wide and he was jabbering excitedly "Oh my God, oh my God..." And I don't remember what all he said exactly but I calmed him down and he kept saying that I reminded him of someone, that so-called guru that I mentioned I'd been dreaming about talking to right before the first encounter with the Golden Whirlwind.

I got him talking about how he ended up in jail and it turned out he'd been at a wet T-shirt contest that had turned into an orgy and there were people having sex on the tables. He was still outside in the line trying to get in when the cops raided it and that's how he had gotten arrested—trying to push his way in before the cops broke up the party.

I remember sitting there, looking at the other guys and I realized I could see into their dreams, see images from their lives, and feel their feelings. At one point I remember thinking that maybe I could extend my will and unlock the cell door. But after a few seconds of starting down that path I realized that even if I got it open there was no place to go.

A little later the officer came back. It was actually the Lieutenant who had booked me, and he had been the one knocked aside by the Whirlwind. He came up to the cell door and started a roll call of all the people who were supposed to be in the tank. When he got to my name I didn't answer, because they never did get the whole name right, just parts of it. Also there were people in there whose names he didn't call. It happened twice, he called my name but it wasn't my whole name and I refused to answer. And he was staring at me and I knew that he'd figured out that he didn't have my whole name.

Later he came back with a breakfast menu, at least that's what he said it was; can you believe it? Like you get a choice for breakfast in the tank. He tried to get my name from me again. Then he came back one more time. He looked at me and he said "Sir, I'm really sorry. I'm really sorry for what happened to you." Then he walked away.

Later someone did come with breakfast and I couldn't eat it; the smell made me sick. Somebody said "Here, I'll take it." and I gave it out to share. A couple hours later they came and got a bunch of us. I remember standing in the hallway in the holding area outside the courtroom. We were passing around a cigarette that someone had picked up off the floor.

We lined up in there and went before the judge in groups of two. I remember the guy I went in with, an older guy, hair going gray, dirty clothes, looked like he lived on the street. He told me to just agree with whatever the judge said. He told me, "Don't piss him off, I have to get out of here."

The judge looked at what he had written in front of him. He looked at me and back down at the paper and said, "Six foot six inches and two hundred forty pounds? You're not that big."

I said, "No sir, I'm not."

He said, "That's what these idiots wrote down."

I remember thinking "No wonder I appeared threatening." He asked me questions like, "It says here drunk and disorderly. Were you drunk and disorderly?"

And I thought about it. I wasn't drunk, I was just weeping. So I guess I was disorderly, eh? So I looked at him and said, "Yes". There was really no point in arguing about it.

"Do you have any money?"

I said, "No, I don't have any money."

"And what are you going to do?"

I said, "I got a bus ticket to St. Louis."

Then he said, "Well, you be out of town within 24 hours and don't come back."

And I said, "Yes sir." I got my stuff back from the property room and they let me out on the street.

The dialogue years later:

I sat for a long time.

Q: "What, you got nothing? You got nothing to say?"

M: "I want to think for a minute."

Q: "OK."

M: "OK. What was it? Twice now, the Golden Whirlwind. What was it?"

Q: "I didn't know. In all the research and reading I did in the next few years I tried to track it down following the trail of the Release of the Kundalini Serpent literature. The description of that was fairly common in lots of literature out of the Eastern Religions and so I figured that by tracking that down I'd find information on the Whirlwind because the Whirlwind was what caused the Release in me.

I found paintings of the whirlwind in sacred art, and read descriptions of it in sacred literature and I didn't like what I found at all. Those books described it as The Enlightenment. Not some Satori or Illumination, mind you, but the big one.

My first reaction was of course 'No way'. I had done nothing to deserve that, no years of suffering in monasteries practicing austerities and self-disciplines. No sitting under a Bo Tree for 40 days and nights. But the books said that those paths weren't the only way it could happen. Some said it could happen by accident, like the Kundalini Release could sometimes happen by accident.

I remember also in my studies that somewhere I came across a book that referred to a master/student relationship that existed in certain Tibetan monasteries and that one of the chief jobs of the Master, as the student was nearing the Enlightenment, was to watch over the student when the energy in that golden whirlwind form would come down. It's one of the few references I've ever seen to this and I don't remember what book it was. I don't have the book anymore, but I remember that the chief job of the Master in that moment was to keep a being that hid in that energy away from the student so that just the energy of the Enlightenment came in.

And then I discovered another significant reference to a Golden Whirlwind when I was going back through the story in my mind, trying to figure out with research all those elements of prophecy in the story. I found it in the Book of Job. In that book, the one they call 'God' appeared to Job as a Golden Whirlwind, in some translations anyway. In other translations it's just a whirlwind."

M: "Jesus."

Q: "Well, no. Although some of the esoteric Christian literature said that Jesus wrote the Book of Job in his previous incarnation as Elijah.

Have you read it? The Book of Job? A fine story about God and Satan making a bet on Job's fidelity by destroying his life and murdering his children. Oh, in the end, after Job has his crisis of faith, and God proves his might, he gives Job back his life with new children.

Nobody ever asks about how the children felt about being murdered by God. Nobody ever cared about what his wife thought."

M: "Bizarre. The whole thing, I mean."

Q: "Yes. East and West in one image, the same image emerging from legend from the major cultures across the world, a form of pure energy concealing an entity. Even some tribal cultures have tales of the Golden Whirlwind.

Once again, you have to remember, I didn't know any of this stuff at the time. I knew that the Golden Whirlwind was something big, and something powerful, and something significant, but I really had no idea what the significance could have been. What I knew was that I wasn't significant, personally, and that meant that I couldn't trust any of it. And I never have trusted any of it.

The truth is that I still don't know for sure, anyway. It's not like some expert or master has ever appeared in my life and confirmed any of it. I just live with it.

But here's the thing: once my research showed me that these things could be real, and had precedent, and what they might mean, then the probability that they were real went way up for me, because I had the experience without any foreknowledge of the possibility of the experience. I couldn't have imagined it, which is what I was worried about. I had to know that I didn't just make it all up. I had to know that I wasn't delusional, and that this stuff was real.

And another thing that the research showed me is that these kinds of things usually don't happen. Normally, nobody would have been saved from what might have been a skull fracture like I was. They would have just died there on the bench. People just don't get saved by Golden Whirlwinds every day, or go through the Release of the Kundalini Serpent like I did.

But it happened. And I still don't know why. Or why me.

And there's one more part to it. If these things happened, they had to happen in accordance with Natural Law. One thing I'm sure of it that there's a lot of stuff about Natural Law that we don't understand, and maybe a lot more that we don't know about.

I never could understand how it was that I was able to find my way to the Golden Whirlwind entity the first time, when it was out there looking at those two stars. Stuff like that wasn't supposed to happen either. People have dedicated their lives to searching for that opening and never found it. Years later, out in the wilderness, I was sitting there with my books on the table contemplating that question: 'How could that have happened?' in a place of internal inquiry, you know what I mean?"

I nodded yes.

Q: "So I was holding this question and a visual answer appeared. It was of a man walking down a beach, wearing a ragged white cotton shirt and trousers. His hair was long and wild and he looked Hindu, but he wasn't in India. The audio said 'Indonesia'. It looked like a beach in Bali.

He started talking to me through the vision, is what happened; wild gestures, yelling and waving his arms, in his own language. I understood it, because I heard it in English. What he said was:

'I left it for you. I found the door but I wouldn't go through so I left it. I knew someone would come along and use it.'

And then the vision collapsed."

M: "What do you mean by Natural Law?"

Q: *"Really? Didn't they teach you anything?"*

M: "Yeah, I know what they mean, but what do you mean?"

Q: *"I mean the same thing. Nature is arranged in certain ways and not other ways. And there are consequences to going contrary to the ways Nature is arranged. And there are lots of sayings about this, like 'Don't piss into the wind.'"*

M: "Well, unless you want to accidentally piss on the guy taking a leak next to you."

Q: *"What?"*

M: "Or like, 'Don't shit uphill.'"

Q: *"Wait. What?*

M: "Cause it will always get on your heels. I got another one: Don't masturbate with toothpaste.'"

Q: *"Never mind. I don't want to know."*

12

SACRIFICE

I got on the next bus to St. Louis. I was in a state of both fear and bliss at the same time. Oh, and all the feelings and dreams and internal dialogues of those around me were back in my head. I started to feel a little ill. I was shivering, I hadn't eaten anything in a couple of days.

Sitting in the seats in front of me were a man and a woman. The man was dressed in this kind of pimped out style from the times; bright clothes and a broad brimmed velvet hat, and this woman was 5, maybe 6, years younger than him, dressed kind of college kid casual in a hooded sweatshirt, t-shirt, and jeans. I started listening to what he was saying to her.

He was going on and on about how he was a warlock, and that he was a member of a coven. He wanted her to come and join them on their Sabbath ceremony. He was really laying it on thick, talking about how he had power, how they had sexual rituals to build the power and what all they did at the rituals. He talked about how nobody ever messed with them because of all the power they could make and about how they could use it to get whatever they wanted.

It was just one of the most amazing pickup spiels I had ever heard.

She was being resistant but politely curious. I could feel she was a little afraid. It was just really weird.

I remember as I got more ill I started coughing, and accidentally coughed on him. He turned and gave me a dirty look, breaking the almost hypnotic hold he had on the girl. He turned back around with a kind of "Where was I?" expression on his face.

Suddenly I was having a vision. It was someone who looked like us being held down on a rock out on an island on one of the rivers and there were two other guys holding him down. One of them was the guy who drove me back to town after that first meeting with the group. The other was this huge guy doing most of the holding on the guy who looked like us. This guy was crying and yelling and struggling and then suddenly I was inside him, looking up at the other two. The guy I knew from the group took out a knife and gave it to the big guy and he slit the throat of the man on the rock. And as the knife crossed his throat I could feel the knife cutting my throat from side to side. I felt it in my body as if it were happening to me.

And then, since my awareness was in this guy, I spoke through his mouth and said "Are you quite finished yet?" They stepped back in amazement and fear and let go of the dead guy and then I animated the guy's body and got him up off the rock and walked him to the edge of the clearing where I left him and his body collapsed.

I thought it might have been you.

On the bus I kept getting more ill and I withdrew into myself as far as I could, as if by making myself small the evil all around me wouldn't find me.

Because, when I thought about it, I realized that they would figure it out. They'd figure it out that whoever animated the guy they killed was the one they were looking for. Now they'd know they'd killed the wrong guy.

The dialogue years later:

Q: *"No rest for the weary, eh?"*

M: "Yeah, really. Did you know there was a third?"

Q: *"Yup. Well, at least I figured there was. Maybe more. Too many stories about us for there to have been only two."*

M: "So, suddenly there's warlocks and witches and human sacrifice and all that stuff, that stuff that also supposedly doesn't exist. What was going on?"

Q: *"Well, now, wait a minute. They're not necessarily related. Remember, it was the 70's, and there was resurgence of interest in neo-paganism and witchcraft. Those people don't do human sacrifice. It's a whole subject that I've looked into, looking for meaningful connections but I haven't found any. The greatest likelihood was that the guy on the bus wasn't even for real, he was just running a pick up line on the girl. Worse, it might not even have been a coven he was recruiting her for, just as likely it was his stable. For me the experience, the way it felt, was more about the proximity of something evil than about some simple nature-based sex magic.*

And what happened on the rock? That wasn't human sacrifice; there was nothing ritual about it. It was murder.

That's what it was about: the proximity of evil."

13

AN INTERLUDE OF STRANGENESS

So I made it to St. Louis and went by the luggage room and got my knapsack. Everything was intact, it was all there. I went back to the hotel and the guy behind the desk smiles real big and says, "There you are, Sir. We've been expecting you. We've got the same room for you." And he gave me the same room at the hotel that I had the previous two times. It was totally weird. What if he'd been waiting for you? Or one of the others? I crashed, and spent the night sweating out the fever.

In the morning I slept in and about lunchtime I went around the corner to have a sandwich and a beer. That afternoon it started to turn strange again. There were a bunch of guys in suits and ties in there eating lunch and drinking beers, jackets hanging on the back of their chairs, sleeves rolled up. It turned out that they were young stockbrokers and they were on their way to an investment seminar. I got to talking and joking with them. They decided that they liked me so much that they'd invite me to go along. So I did. But I didn't have the right clothes so we went back to this one guy's apartment and he loaned me a shirt and tie and some slacks but he didn't have a jacket that fit me. I went along to that seminar but we were so drunk it was all some of us could do to just sit there and not throw up.

Afterwards we all went out and drank some more. Then the group broke up and the guy whose clothes I had and I went back to my hotel room so I could pick up some more money and change my clothes. Basic stockbroker wasn't my look. It was one of those encounters with someone new when you just talk nonstop about all kinds of things, but inevitably, alcohol leads to philosophy. One of the things we'd been talking about were my answers to those three questions.

Back in my hotel room was a paper that I'd been writing that had the solution to a math problem that had never been solved before and the solution turned out to be the key to the answer to one of those questions. It was the key to the answer of the question about significance; it was the key to significance. And the paper contained some of the other things about the answers to the other questions. For some reason I had hidden the paper in the room, underneath the wooden cover that was on top of the radiator. And I had a bunch of other papers and stuff scattered on the dresser.

I went into the bathroom to take a leak and all the sudden, when he thought I wasn't looking, the guy started tearing my room apart looking for that paper. He was rifling through things with this glazed and unfocused expression on his face, moving things around, opening drawers. I came out of the bathroom and stood there watching and he didn't pay any attention to me at all. Of course, he didn't find the paper where I'd hidden it. So I asked him "What are you doing?" He snapped back into awareness of himself in the room and said, "I don't have a clue. Let's get the fuck out of here." So we got out of there.

Ahh, I don't know, you know? All day this crazy feeling was building in me, this crazy energy. So much stuff happened to me, so much stuff had been done to me, I started to feel like I had to do, you know? I felt like I had to act, or act out, that I'd been too passive.

I remember we went over to his girlfriend's apartment and right away she took a shine to me. So we decided to go out for more beer and we got in her car, a little Volkswagen beetle, and they let me drive. I was driving like a crazy person. They were trying to give me directions to the bar and I was driving the wrong way down a one-way four-lane street at fifty miles an hour and taking corners on two wheels. So we pulled into the parking lot from the alley out back of this little bar, the last open bar downtown.

We went in past some other cars and there was this beautiful police motorcycle parked there on the edge of a little slope. I was so full of craziness that as we walked past that motorcycle I reached down and grabbed it and flipped it. It rolled over down the slope and we went on into the bar. We ordered beers and a six pack to go. We were standing at the bar drinking and having a good time and this girl is liking me all the more for being crazy and in comes this cop, same size and build and looks as the one that had arrested me in Memphis. He came storming in, all puffed up, and yelled "Who flipped my bike? I know whoever did it is in this bar." Meanwhile the six pack had come up, and we finished paying and just walked right past him ignoring him, talking to each other and laughing, completely nonchalant.

We went back to her place and her boyfriend was so drunk she had to put him to bed. She closed the bedroom door and I was leaning on the wall. She came over to me and put her arms around me and pressed herself up against me, kissed me and said something like, "He's out but we could still have a lot of fun." And I thought about it. I almost took her up. And then I said, "Nah, nah, darlin', I need you to stay with him tonight because he's been through a lot, trust me." And then I left, taking all that craziness with me instead of running it out with her.

The dialogue years later:

M: "So what's all this have to do with the story?"

Q: *"Mostly I'm just telling the story, warts and all. But there are a couple of things. First, the guy scrambling through my stuff wasn't in his right mind. By which I mean, that somebody else was in his mind, driving him to do things he wasn't aware he was doing. It was a warning that weird stuff was afoot, improbable reality that smelled like magic and power. It had happened before back on the River, remember? When that deckhand had asked me about going through initiation. Another warning of things to come, an indicator of the invisible circling around.*

Second, about the cop and the motorcycle. Another example of physically identical people hundreds of miles apart. I'd had a feeling when I flipped the bike. Honestly I was moved by that craziness, that wildness and the need to do something for what had been done to me. The fact that they were identical showed me there was something right in what I'd done. The cops had done me a little bit wrong back in Memphis. They knew it, that's why the one apologized.

Third, I was beginning to attract attention from women again."

He grinned.

14

ABDUCTION

The next morning I went down to the Union Hall, I don't know, about 10 or 11 o'clock. After taking care of whatever business, paying my dues I think, and talking with the steward to make sure he would remember me, I went out to the waiting room. I suddenly started to have this rising feeling of terror while I was standing there in the office. Sheer terror of something drawing closer, rising up and gripping me so hard it was hard to breathe. I could feel that it was coming down the street and I was up on the 10th floor. I could feel it; I could feel it when the source of the terror walked into the building.

There was this other deckhand there, who looked remarkably like a cute girl that I had a crush on eight or nine years before; a girl who'd been really sweet to me, you know, but it had never gone anywhere. Same skin and eyes, same long straight dark hair. But I had really trusted her and I had been talking to this deckhand, striking up a conversation with him, and I felt the same kind of trust toward him, because of what he looked like, the same feeling that I had felt towards her.

But as I felt that terror rising, the terror started to show up as trembling in my voice. He could hear it and he started getting nervous.

It looked like he could feel the terror, too, and he suddenly said, "I don't have time to talk right now. I've got to go somewhere."

I said, "Where're you going?"

And the guy says, "Well, I'm not gonna tell you."

By this time it was clear we could both feel the evil coming up in the elevator, getting closer, and I was close to panic.

So I said, "Well, how you gonna get there?"

And he said, "Well, well, I'm going down the stairs. I'm not hanging out here any longer," and he ran out of the office and down the hallway.

And I followed him, chasing him down the hall and then down the stairs as the evil thing was riding up the elevator. I could feel it when we passed it going up while we went down. We came running down the stairs, burst out into the lobby, and I could feel it step out of the elevator and realize I was gone. We ran out the front doors onto the sidewalk. He ran right and I ran left.

Suddenly, right there on the street in a car that was identical to the car that I had been driven back to town in from the first meeting with the group, were two guys. The one looked identical to the guy from the group and had been on the island in the vision. The other was the big guy from the island. They were the same guys from the murder on the rock. Or two guys who looked just like them.

They saw me and shouted at me, "Hey! You there! Wait a minute, stop! Stop!" and they went to unbuckle their seatbelts, and get out of the car and because of the interlock the engine stalled. The big guy tried to get out, got his door open but got tangled in the seatbelt and the other guy put the car in park and tried to get it started again. Both of them were still yelling at me but I kept running. I cut into an alley and then into another alley and took back ways, sneaking back to my hotel.

The further I ran the less I could feel that terror from the Union

Hall, but I was pretty badly scared. These were the bad guys and they had found me.

I packed up my stuff, waited a few hours until after dark, then took a cab across the river, and started hitchhiking. I had to run from these people and the terror. I had to go back home and see if my friends were all right. And to warn my parents and tell them what happened to me because I knew I had to disappear.

The dialogue years later:

M: "What was coming up in the elevator?"

Q: *"I have no idea. I think I was more terrified by whatever it was than I'd ever been in my life, up until that moment. More terrified than by the demon in the corner that night near Cairo."*

M: "So do you think the murder on the rock was real or prescient?"

Q: *"I thought at the time that it was real. I still do. I felt the knife, in total sensation, as it opened my throat. I don't think I could have imagined that. I think they knew I was still alive, and they were seeking me out to finish the job. Only this time they were following somebody, this evil presence, who could track me, and whom I could feel when they got close enough.*

I think they were going to take me right off the street, and given the power of what I felt, I had no chance but to run. Sitting there in the hotel room I knew I had to move fast and move small. And in those days you could hitch-hike anywhere."

M: "Why didn't they find you at the hotel?"

Q: *"I don't know for sure. They knew I worked on the River, so they would figure out to check at the Union Hall. But they never knew where I was staying, remember? I'd been suspicious at the first meeting and I'd had the guy drop me off downtown and I walked back to my room. And remember, there was something weird going on at the hotel. The clerks kept giving me the same room, and were even anticipating the day of my return. I don't think the clerks were in on it, but I think something might have been influencing the clerks. Don't know what, though, and as much as I'd like to assume it was benevolent, I can't. It was just more weirdness. It's harder to find somebody in a crowd, too. I sat in that room, lights off, as still and indrawn as possible, waiting for a couple hours past dark, waiting until I felt the coast was clear. I believe they would have found me there if I had stayed much longer.*

What I know is that there are people who are strong enough to take over the mind of another person. Not many, but some. I also know there are invisible things, things that are normally invisible, that is, that can do the same thing. Some of them may be benign; at least I'd like to think so. But I'm also close to certain that they're all constrained by something, I guess you'd call it their 'self-interest'. They're all constrained to act in their self-interest, and whichever side their interest coincides with, that's where they'll act. I've never been able to trust the invisibility though, and the taking over an individual's mind, no matter what side they're on."

M: "Invisibility huh? How's that, and how can you see them if they're invisible?"

Q: *"Well, you can't see them if they're invisible, right? Wake up. They can be heard, sometimes, and sensed, like in touch. And felt, sometimes as a pressure, but sometimes also as an emotion; an emotion that suddenly appears inside you, but you know it isn't your own emotion. It's suddenly there, but you know the emotion didn't arise inside you. You have to really be paying attention to catch it when it happens. Sometimes the emotion will influence your thoughts, sometimes your own feelings, and sometimes it will even move you to action. A being like this can be standing there right next to you, invisibly, and projecting emotions into you."*

M: "Why?"

Q: *"To influence your choices, and your behavior. And sometimes when you are feeling the emotion, or dealing with the consequences of your actions on the emotional level, it will tune into your feelings, and share them, resonate with them. Feed on them."*

M: "I am disbelieving you."

Q: "And there's more than one kind. Sometimes it's the dead. Sometimes it's someone alive and dreaming. Sometimes it's someone who's projected a higher body but doesn't have the power to make it visible, or chooses not to. Sometimes it's a Light-Bender, a being who can project the image of what is behind it around to its front, so when you look at it you see as if you were seeing through it to what is actually in its background.

I remember one time I was about to kiss a girl, a girl I really wanted to kiss, but probably shouldn't have. We got in close to each other, but suddenly I felt a huge surge of excitement rising from behind her off to the right, an excitement that matched the excitement I was feeling and amplified it. When I looked there was a wavering image in the outline of something man-shaped. When it felt me seeing it, it snapped out my vision.

She said, "It felt like there was something that really wanted us to make that kiss. Something was pushing us to kiss. It felt like a demon."

And I said, "Don't know that I'd call it a demon but, yes, there was something, standing right there, behind your shoulder. That's why we're not going to."

She said she was OK with that. That was the last time I saw her. A shame too, in a way. We would have been great lovers. For about a week anyway.

More disbelief?"

M: "Wait, wait, you're telling me there's invisible stuff going on all the time around us, right?"

Q: "No, I'm not. There might be invisible stuff going on all the time but I'm not talking about stuff. Sometimes there's invisible beings going on around us. Most of the time not. Why would there be? What's going on that's so important in your life that something would spend the energy to be invisible around you? What's going on with you that something would want to spend time around you resonating with your field?

Remember that all these things have to behave in a way that's congruent with their own interest. It's both an opportunity and a constraint."

M: "So you ran."

Q: "Yes. Well, I'd call it a strategic escape. It had all become very serious, and very real. I didn't know if I could fight that terror, and I didn't want to try. I was just one man."

15

Running While Dead

That's what it was like in my head after that morning on the street: "Get out now or you're dead." The first place I had to go to was the southern mountains where some friends of mine were staying. It was partly because some of the minor characters in what I had just been through had physical archetypal resemblances to my friends. You know the guy who said, "It looks like you're getting your initiation into the mysteries," looked like somebody, the hotel clerk looked like somebody, people who would smile at me on the street looked like somebody. Mostly though it was because they didn't look anything like the main characters; different physical archetypes completely.

So I went to them first because it seemed safer. I hoped to lose them, shake the ones looking for me off my trail so they wouldn't follow me to my folks. I moved without stopping, one ride right after another. I caught good rides, got there quick, got way out in the country. But I could still feel the others following with the same sense I felt the evil coming up the elevator, just not as strong. I could feel when I was ahead of them, I could feel when I got behind them, I could feel when they overshot me, I could feel when they lost me and I could feel when they'd locked back on to my trail. I spent a fair amount of time standing off to the side of the road, waiting in the brush until I felt the coast was clear. The Chorus was constantly feeding me information about whether it was OK or not, not that I believed it. It was crazy-making. I took some indirect roads, too. The thing from the Union Hall that terrified me wasn't travelling with them, but was guiding them, those two, it seemed, who'd tried to take me on the street.

When I got to the mountains I told my friends the story of what had been happening to me. Mostly I just triggered disbelief. One of my friends offered to take me up north to where my parents and my other friends were, so we drove. I had him give me some of his old clothes to wear. I stopped wearing all my own clothes because they were close and they'd seen me. I wore a hat, I got a hat that didn't belong to me. We drove up the mountains on the back roads in a 1954 International one-ton flatbed truck. I could feel my trackers cutting my trail all the way north. It was overcast often, with fogs or light showers, and that seemed to make it feel harder for them, as if the weather was covering my trail, like it had been on the river.

The first place we went was to my mother's house. While we were there I could feel them getting closer and closer. While she fed us I told her the short version of the story. I described what they looked like and I warned her they were following me.

Then we left there and went to look for my other friends. I wanted to warn them, too, because I felt the trackers were getting close and we didn't have much time. Here's how close they were: within 15 minutes of leaving my mother's house somebody matching the physical description of the driver in the car in St. Louis showed up knocking at her door with a clipboard in his hand, pretending to be a surveyor for the power company.

Her cat freaked out. My mother stood there at the door, bending over trying to keep the cat from leaping out and attacking this guy. He was bending over trying to get her to look in his eyes and she remembered my story and refused to do that. She refused to do that and suddenly she couldn't control the cat anymore. It exploded through the door, leaped onto his thigh with all four paws and dug in. The guy screamed and swatted at the cat, giving my mother the chance to slam the door. She told him to get out of there; she was calling the cops.

At the same time about 10 miles away my buddy and I were driving down the road in the International and there came my friends, P and F, walking down the road. Suddenly the overcast sky becomes dark and, boom, thunder broke. The rain poured down in a curtain so heavy you couldn't see anything further away than 6 feet. I had told my friend earlier that rain seemed to cover the trail. My buddy turned to me and said, "I thought maybe you were crazy but I believe you now."

We quickly got them in the truck with us and went to someplace safer in the rain—we ducked into a nearby church with an open door. I told them the story. F said yes, he had felt those little swirling whirlwinds trying to get into his head and make him think thoughts. He was really fucking angry at me. "How dare you get involved in anything that would put me at risk like that," he said.

They weren't happy to see me, these two friends. We spent the whole night driving around. We had to keep moving until the trail was wiped out. We got invited to a couple of parties at different points in the night and later we headed back towards my friends' house to sleep because I could feel that we'd lost the ones following us in the rain.

Just before dawn it stopped raining. I was so exhausted that I had to go to sleep right away. On the back of his truck my friend had a short stack of 4 x 8 sheets of plywood. I got him to agree to put a tarp over me and strap me down on top of the stack. With my feet sticking out the back, I fell asleep.

We were driving through this one small town right around sunrise. Somebody had come out onto the street, and had been standing there when we drove by and called the cops, claiming he'd seen a bunch of hippies hauling a dead man through town. (Laughter, and the recorder stops for a time). We got out of town and up on the bypass and were rolling along. A state trooper came up behind us, lights flashing, and pulled us over. He came up to the window and said, "We've had a complaint that you're hauling the dead without a license."

My friend said, "What? He ain't dead. Here, I'll show you." He got out and pushed me on the shoulder and called my name. I was dead to the world and I didn't wake up; I didn't move, I didn't answer, Nothing.

So he pulled back the tarp and hit me good on the shoulder a couple of times and said, "Wake up! Wake up, you son of a bitch, and show this man you ain't dead."

That woke me up enough so that I moaned at him and said, "I ain't dead", real slow and drawn out. I felt like I was reaching up out of a long dark cave into a world too fast to care about. My friend got to laughing really hard and asked the cop to write up a warning ticket so he could show it to all his friends because nobody would ever believe it.

Later that day I had my friend take me down to my father's house. I told my father and his wife the story and then I left. I told him I didn't know when I'd see them again. Then I spent one more evening with my friends. The thunderstorms came in again and every time one of us moved, it seemed, the lightning would flash.

I knew it was time to leave under cover of the storms. We got up early in the morning and didn't say goodbye. So my friend and I drove back down south. And from there I caught a ride with a young family that was migrating West. On our way we stopped in Memphis and I got my sea bag from up in the rafters of the shed on the docks there on the river.

It was the end of friendship. I didn't think I would see any of those people again. And I couldn't sense my pursuers anywhere close. I could feel them searching but it was faint, like listening to hounds running the wrong way, and I was afraid to linger too long on sensing them, in case that opened a door for them to sense me. I would touch in only briefly and then be gone.

I thought I'd try to go back to school at least while I figured out what to do next. It was on the other side of the country, and my pursuers had no idea about that part of my life, and I couldn't feel them tracking me. And when I got back there it was very strange.

The school had assumed that I wasn't coming back and I didn't have a room on campus assigned to me and none of the loans and finances had been arranged.

I had sent money back early in the summer to mechanic friends of mine to go buy a truck from a professor for me, a 1941 Ford flatbed. They spent the money getting drunk because they figured I wasn't coming back either. The professor had sold the truck to someone else because he figured I wasn't coming back.

The one mechanic looked at me and said, "We figured you weren't coming back," and the other mechanic said, "Hell, I thought you were gonna go get yourself killed somewhere."

When I asked them "Why?" they shrugged their shoulders, neither of them had anything to say, except "I don't know," grinning at me foolishly.

I want to stop here a minute and think about what I want to say next.

The dialogue years later:

M: "What was that like, coming back to someplace where nobody thought you'd return? Worse, people thought you were likely dead?"

Q: *"Well, it made me sad. I think I probably felt a little dead. And unseen, like a ghost. And angry. These people had given me their word they would do what I needed them to do while I was gone. The school itself in particular made me angry. I was able to browbeat them into letting me back into class, but I had nowhere to stay, and I had to borrow all the money to attend.*

I can't believe, sort of, that I was still trying to return to a 'normal' life after all I'd been through.

I was trying to live the life of a regular guy, believing I had out-run the bad guys, and I started doing the research into what had happened to me. I believed that, whatever it was, whatever the story was, that it was done.

Or that it was done with me, and in a weird way, since I didn't die despite everybody believing that I had gone off to die, that both their belief in my death and my return was a kind of proof that it was over.

But I have to tell you that I was grieving and raging all the time. And my mind was always on, not just re-running the details of the story, but trying to deal with the sensations and the feelings of being around all these people again. Feeling their feelings, sensing their sensations. Catching little bits of their internal dialogue. Dreaming their dreams. That may have been the worst part, dreaming their dreams.

You might be amazed, well, maybe you wouldn't be, if you knew just how insipid most people's internal lives are. Sex, food. Or insidious, seeking revenge. Not a lot of thinking, just free association driven by whatever they happen to be feeling at the moment.

But their dreams, oh man, so pitiful. The waking life of the people was enough to make me question my love for them, that love which had led me to deal for their freedom. But their dreams just filled me with compassion for their suffering.

It was different on the river, and when I was hitch-hiking. There were way fewer people around and I was always moving. Those two factors, especially the constant motion, had made it a little easier to get through the days and nights, but now that I was in one place, it was bad.

And dreaming prescient dreams every night; not big things always, but sometimes. Lots of times it was stuff like the next day's newspaper head-line or what the clerk at the gas station would say to me when I bought something.

I began to feel trapped by it. Where's the freedom in living a life where everything you do is from something you've dreamed about the night before? What's the point?

I wondered if this was what they meant by 'the price of man's freedom was mine,' now that nothing I could do or would live through would ever be free from having been determined the night before. Or maybe it was just a consequence of the Kundalini Release. I had no way of telling. So, for me, the task each day was to find the courage to do something, to move against the pressure of my growing despair."

16

A HOLE IN THE SKY

So there I was, no place to live, no truck, and everybody thinking I was either dead or never going to come back. Things continued to be very strange.

But I still had friends there. One of them let me stay in the camper that he parked on the street in front of his house. I was still dreaming all the time, even when I was awake, still seeing futures, possibilities, things that were likely to happen in the future. I decided somewhere along in there that all these dreams that had that certain quality to them that made me suspect they were likely to come true at some point in the future were things that shouldn't come true as a matter of principle, that the future should not be fixed.

I realized that these dreams of the future were "presa vus," prescient dreams where you remember the dream, unlike "deja vus" where you only have the feeling that you were there before. These dreams were like prophecies, and like the prophecies, warnings about what would happen if some change wasn't made.

I came to believe that the only good prophecy was a dead prophecy, so to speak. And that I had to take steps to change something so that every one of those dreams, even the dreams that seemed to me like good ones, should never come true as I had dreamed them. The Chorus was not pleased, and argued with me about this.

I remember one afternoon I had been out in my friend's backyard burning some clothes in his trash barrel, clothes that I would never wear again, or any clothes like them, because changing my clothes was the only element I could figure out to change in some of those dreams of the future.

His wife had seen me out in the backyard doing that. She was look-ing at me through the kitchen window like I was crazy, burning perfectly good clothes, and I figured I'd better give it a break, so I picked up the unburned clothes. I went around front and stepped into his camper when suddenly dogs began to howl. First a few dogs and then more dogs. Then suddenly it seemed like all of the dogs in the city were howling on this bright sunny afternoon, which is something I'd never heard of dogs doing before. It was literally hair-raising.

I stepped back outside to see what was going on and looked around. I looked up in the sky and suddenly a hole appeared in the sky off to the North. This hole grew until it was about four hand breadths across and another sky appeared behind this hole. The clouds in my sky would come to the edge of this hole and disappear, and then reappear on the other side of the hole. But the clouds in this other sky were going in a different direction and they would appear on the inside edge and then disappear when they got to the far side. And the color of the sky inside the hole was a different shade of blue than my sky outside the hole.

Then kind of a golden light appeared in the shape of a wide bar or a line but with one end on the left up-turned in a curve and the other end on the right curved downward. And this light hung there in the sky for several minutes with the dogs howling, and I remember thinking, "Well, good then. Maybe they won't destroy us after all."

Then the light faded and the hole closed up and the dogs stopped howling and the sky went back to being one sky.

That evening my friend came home from work and we were sitting there with his family eating supper. He said to me, "Did you hear those dogs today? We heard them at work and we went outside and stood there and looked. There was something really strange in the sky. Did you see it? You ever seen anything like that? What was that?"

I nodded yes and said, "It was a hole in the sky."

He said, "What? A hole in the sky? Really? You ever heard of such a thing?"

I said, "Yeah I've heard of them but they don't happen often."

He said, "What was that light?"

I said, "I don't know, some kind of sign maybe."

His response was a thoughtful "Well, what do you know…"

But his wife was looking at me funny and their eyes met, in that silent communication way. That night she asked him to ask me to leave. So I was back looking for a place to live again the next day.

I remember how crazy this all was. I couldn't understand what was happening, why everybody thought that I was either going to end up dead or simply not return. It was as if I had no place anywhere. I decided to go on out to the highway and on the edge of town there was a gypsy woman who told fortunes. I went up to the door, knocked, and she let me in.

Her daughter was sitting there in the living room watching TV and I told the woman that there were some things going on and I wanted to see if the cards could show me anything about them. She took me into the kitchen, sat me down, and told me the price. Her daughter came and stood in the doorway, leaned on the frame with her arms crossed, and watched as her mother got out a deck of playing cards, which was what she used instead of a tarot deck.

She laid out the cards and looked at the spread, clucked her tongue, and rolled her eyes back in her head. She clucked her tongue some more, and sucked on her teeth. Then she said, "Do not worry, you will have help."

She said, "The cards tell me you also need a good woman. There is my daughter there. She is available, and I can tell you are a good man."

I looked at her daughter and her daughter smiled, and I smiled back and her mother said, "No, no, I was just kidding. Thank you very much. You can pay me now." I paid her and she showed me out.

I remember in these times a friend of mine who had physical archetypes almost identical to A fell completely in love with me, I mean claws out in love. She invited me over to dinner and we were talking. She was telling me how much she loved me. She got up and went into the kitchen to do something with supper. I had an intuition to quietly get up and follow her. After a moment I caught her stirring her hair into the soup and casting rhyming love spells over it.

When I challenged her on it, it was as if she woke up from sleep, and she said she had no idea why she was doing it. Then she broke down in tears.

It occurred to me then that they might be getting close.

The dialogue years later:

M: "So what was going on there?"

Q: *"Which? Where?"*

M: "These people who would do these things around you, things that obviously weren't normal for them, and then you call them and they come back to the present like they'd been off asleep somewhere?"

Q: *"When I watched it in the hotel room the word that came to me in the moment was 'possession'."*

M: "Yeah, but by what?"

Q: *"I couldn't tell. Sometimes it seemed like the bad guys, sometimes it seemed more neutral somehow. But what I knew was that things were still happening along the lines of physical and archetypal resemblance. I think maybe resemblance made it easier for a takeover to happen.*

What this meant to me was that anybody, particularly anybody near me, who had resemblances to any of the archetypes of those other people would be susceptible to being overtaken. But what could I do? Abandon them? Run away? No, they were my friends, I had to stay and protect them, bring them back when they were overtaken.

But then again, if I wasn't around they wouldn't be at risk at all, would they?

But it would happen anywhere I went, so I began to make plans to get away from people, just disappear altogether."

M: "So anybody around you could be overtaken at any time."

Q: *"Yes. Now that I wasn't moving, anyway."*

M: "You were very dangerous to be around."

Q: *"Yeah. Lots of girls like danger, though."*

M: "What?"

Q: *"I'm just saying. It was a good time for me in that way. So long as I could keep my act together and not burst into tears, or run off raging into the night."*

M: "Umm, yeah, alright then. About this next thing, you know I have to ask."

Q: *"Go ahead then. Ask with your own self. Your true self. And then listen with it."*

M: "What was the hole in the sky, and what was the, what did you call it? The sign?"

Q: *"I described what I saw. It was a hole, a portal that opened to a different sky, a different blue, with different winds and different clouds. It was like looking into another world, a world normally hidden from ours. If I were simple-minded, instead of just being simple, I'd say it was an opening into Heaven.*

It took only a little research to discover what the sign was. It was a golden Yod, the tenth letter of the Hebrew alphabet, the number 10, the beginning, the Aleph made manifest, a symbol of deep mythological and Qabbalistic meaning. It is the first letter of the Tetragrammaton, the name of God, in the Bible."

M: "Uh. You're kidding."

Q: *"What? Oh, screw you man. What makes you think I would fucking kid about something like that? Wake the fuck up, Matthews, and try to understand. I told you to listen with your own true self, and I think you better pay attention."*

M: "Look, I'm sorry. I apologize. I just don't know what it means, but I'm afraid I do know what it means. And I don't know what that means either."

Q: *"So tell me what you think it means."*

M: "I think that whatever happened to you, whatever it was you were involved in, attracted some way high level attention. And whatever else it might mean, at least it means that the higher attention was present."

Q: *"You know what else it might mean? In those myths there is the story of God putting his bow in the sky, as a symbol that he would never destroy the people again. The common belief is that it was a rainbow, but not the esoteric belief. There is an esoteric belief that it was a flaming Yod."*

M: "Okay."

Q: "You said you were afraid you knew what it meant. And why does that make you afraid?"

M: "Because it means that this stuff is real. All this myth, and these histories, and those books at the basis of Judaism, Christianity, and Islam. That stuff is all real."

Q: "Well, not all of it. There's a lot of stuff that's made up. Lots of other stuff that's been obscured, and obscured deliberately.

But there was definitely something real going on.

It scares me too. It still does, because as much as I've figured out, I still don't really know. I'm a little guy, some bottom dweller in the ocean of the sky trying to figure out what life is like on dry land.

It was my driving question in those days: What is going on here?

I have to say the whole thing also made me really, really angry. What was being done to the people? What were they being used for? And why all this mystery about showing up in the historical record? If these entities and forces were really out there, why so intermittent? Why not stick around and help out a little bit, maybe undo some of the damage that's been done because they weren't around to apply some guidance when the people, as they always do, get it turned around and backwards?

I mean, I know that I don't know a lot, and I know that there's probably lots of appearances and interventions that I don't know about, but you have to admit that the histories of the peoples that have been impacted by their interventions are pretty bloody.

Sometimes it looks to me that no intervention at all might have been better for the people."

17

THE PATH OF THE HEART

It was a crazy time for me. I was angry and terrified and filled with grief. I was raging at the sky. I was weeping uncontrollably and all the time my mind was filled with the images and feelings of others in their suffering close by and far away. My nights were filled with future dreams and the dreams of others. And I was vibrating continuously.

The mechanic buddy who was supposed to have picked up and repaired that old truck for me felt bad enough about what he did to loan me his motorcycle. It was a big 1000 cc bike with a sagging chain and a throttle lock. One night after a few beers with him I took it out on a sandy wind swept back road and wound it way up and set the throttle lock.

My eyes were watering so bad I couldn't see. With the tears streaming back on the sides of my face I stood up on the foot pedals and screamed into the wind, "You sons of bitches, if you are going to let me die then just kill me now. Come on and kill me now." And I stood all the way up and let go of the handlebars.

After maybe a second, though it seemed like more, I took the handlebars again and sat down and unlocked the throttle.

I said to myself, "I guess they want me to live." Then I said to myself, "And that was a really fucking stupid thing to do." The next day I gave him back his motorcycle and I've never been on one since.

Before I had left to work for the summer I had gotten into a partnership on a piece of land south of town. Of course, this partnership fell apart also, but I recall being out there on this land standing on the side of a hill in this craziness. I was wondering what to do and I noticed that whenever I would hold an image of a particular course of action in my mind a different part of my body would respond with a vibrating pulsing energy. The energy would resonate between the image of a path that I could take with a particular region of my body.

There was one image that would make the top of my head pulse, another image that would make my low belly pulse or my solar plexus or my heart or my throat. I had all these different images of different paths and each had a corresponding pulsing sensation in a different part of my body, the pulse linked the image of the path and the region of my body that the path represented.

There was also a variation in the strength of the pulsing in these different paths and regions on my body. The two strongest pulses were in my heart and in the top of my head. I looked down the path for the top of my head. I looked down the path for my heart and the path with the heart was the one I wanted to take least but I also thought that it might take me back toward the center, back toward the place of new beginnings, perhaps.

The more I contemplated which path to take it seemed to me that the path with the heart resonated a little more strongly than the path of the crown, even though I was more strongly drawn to the path with the crown, so I decided to take the path with the heart. And immediately upon making the decision the Chorus said "The path with the heart is the path of greatest suffering."

And with a feeling of mild surprise and some dread, I said, "So be it then." I left the land and started to make some arrangements for setting out on the path with the heart and disappearing down it.

The dialogue years later:

M: "Do you remember what the paths were?"

Q: "Just the two, the path of the Heart, and the path of the Crown. The path of the Crown was a path of retreat from the world, probably to some monastery in India or Tibet. I would have dedicated myself to self-discipline, and learning the techniques of energetic manipulation, learning to control the resonating vibrating energies and use them appropriately."

M: "And the path of the Heart?"

Q: "I told you. It was the path of greatest suffering. It was to disappear into the world."

18

THE HAND

I remember a couple nights later, maybe it was the next night, maybe a week. It had become my intention to disappear. I was lying in bed in a house I was house-sitting because I didn't have a place to live.

Suddenly I felt the sensation of something sliding out of me, sliding out of me from behind and then coming around on my right side, and I could feel this thing turning. Then, appearing above me, was this being that I had merged with back when I had heard the song the stars sing among themselves, right before the first contact with the Golden Whirlwind.

It kept trying, he, it, to put its hand on me, to bring its hand down on me. And I kept trying to resist it. I kept resisting it and kept fighting it. I kept tossing and turning and this force emanated from it, trying to hold me still. It kept trying to bring its hand down on me. The force kept holding me more and more still and the hand kept trying to come down on me.

As I became more and more still, I continued trying to look at it, to look at its face, and it said "Do not look at my face."

Every time I tried to look at its face it would pull its hand back and the force would try to hold me even more still. This happened several times. But I wanted to see who it was. I wanted to see what it was.

I had this sense that the hand was trying to come down on top of my head and I sensed that if that hand came down on me I would forget everything that had happened to me; that it would all be taken away from me and that was something I did not want. I wanted to remember.

Since I didn't want that hand to come down and I wanted to see who this was and I couldn't look at its face directly, I thought of a trick, a ruse, something that I could do that would let me at least look on its face. I tried it once and it didn't work because I was too active so I went completely passive and tried it again in a different way. I succeeded.

I succeeded in looking upon its face just as his hand came down. But instead of coming down on the top of my head the hand came down on my forehead. When the hand came down on my forehead, the vision, and my vision, went black.

(The recorder is paused here)

So the hand came down on me but I had seen its face and I remembered everything.

When it was over and the vision had vanished I calmed down a little bit. It was as if the handprint on my forehead had acted as some kind of a seal, so that I wasn't vibrating so hard all the time and I wasn't seeing things all the time with the same intensity. Some things were obscured then, and the voice of the Chorus was less intense. Sometimes I couldn't hear it at all.

So it changed me and I calmed down a little bit and some of the craziness left me.

The dialogue years later:

I remained silent after we reviewed this, waiting for Q to speak. His eyes were closed, his breathing light, and eventually he sighed, and spoke.

Q: *"This was a strange one. Again, I had no idea what it meant at the time. Years later, living in the wilderness, I encountered a Magician, someone who regularly performed robed devotions to the Light using Grimoire-style rituals. I thought he was an interesting character and he invited me to apprentice to him in his jewelry and precious metal working business. I had accepted, but just to the metal working, not his magical practice. The apprenticeship didn't last long.*

We met, on an early winter afternoon, to finalize the commitments of the apprenticeship, including a plan to work off the costs of my tools and supplies. We lit the first fire of the year in the woodstove to warm up his shop, which was just off a paved road on the way to the nearest town.

I had told him in previous conversations various parts of the story. On this day I told him some of the parts of the story that included the encounters with the Being, as I have described them. On this day I told him the part of the story we just went through.

His reaction was immediate and unequivocal. He said, 'Oh my god, you've been chosen.'

To which I replied, 'What? What do you mean? Chosen for what?'

And he looked within for a moment, and said, 'Never mind. You'll find out in due time.'

I said, 'There must be some mistake.'

He said, 'They don't make mistakes.'

I said, 'It wasn't his intention.'

He said, 'It doesn't matter.'

We continued to talk about it. He asked me what the being looked like, which I described, except for what its face looked like, and he understood why I held that back. And I held back how I had tricked it. We stayed until dark and the fire had burned down.

Later that night, after we'd gone home, there was a chimney fire in the woodstove and his shop burned to the ground. He lost everything.

I will say at this point that disasters like that followed me everywhere, not only in the wilderness years, but for many years thereafter. Unexpected mechanical failures, electrical breakdowns. I learned to fix a lot of things. I couldn't trust mechanical and electrical systems any more than I could trust that somebody who looked like somebody else wouldn't start behaving like somebody else too. I guess maybe it was the other way around though — systems and people couldn't trust being around me.

Bad luck for everyone, it seemed, who had anything to do with me. Maybe that's because they were dealing with somebody who was supposed to be dead, or at least somebody who was very much not where they were supposed to be. All I could think to do was increase my isolation even more. That, and move slowly around electrical stuff. I was off-grid up in the wilderness where I was hiding out; hauling water, gathering firewood for the winter by hand using axes and bow saws. I couldn't afford a chainsaw for years. I had to worry about being around power only when I came into town.

And needless to say, with his shop and his livelihood destroyed, there was no apprenticeship. Working with me was out of the question; it was too dangerous for him, and his family.

When I left the wilderness a few years later I stopped by to see him one last time, to give him the only thing of value I owned at the time, my rifle. This offering of apology and gratitude he accepted with a smile, and brought our relationship to a balanced close. I lost track of him after that; can't find him even today.

Subsequently, my research indicated one of the sources of my friend's pronouncement. Check out Revelation 7:3. One of the legends is that the mark on the forehead will be the imprint of the hand of God.

There's more, of course. Genesis 32, where Jacob wrestles with God, and at the end proclaims that he had looked upon the face of God and his life had been spared. The background legend is that anyone who looks upon the face of God will die."

M: "God? You mean The God? The one everybody believes in?"

Q: "Well, not everybody believes in him, of course."

M: "Oh, yeah. Right. But you're saying that this being you encountered is the God of Judaism, Christianity, and Islam?"

Q: "Nope. I'm not saying that. I think it would be pretty foolish and stupid to say that. What I'm saying is that the being I encountered could be the same being that walked with Abraham, guided Moses, spoke with Jesus, filled John's mind with savage visions, and whispered in the ear of Mohammed. That doesn't make it God. But I can see why somebody might think it was God."

M: "My mind wobbles at the implications. Seriously, I have a wobbling sensation."

Q: "Yeah, mine, too. Hold on to something and the dizziness will pass. I suppose it could have been some other entity. Maybe the Demiurge. Who knows, eh? It could have even been some aspect of myself—a projection out of my own grandiosity. Sure."

He went quiet for a long time. Then he spoke again.

Q: "You know, I've never believed in any of this stuff. I've never identified with it, never identified with some role or status.

And in fact everything that I did was to make sure that all that prophesied stuff never happened, that the people would be free from all that madness. Even so, I may not have been able to stop all of it. Some parts may yet come true, but those parts won't.

And in truth, I cannot imagine that any assembly of the chosen is an assembly where I'd be welcome, especially given that the supposed 'status' was attained by a ruse."

He went quiet again.

Q: *"You know, the Buddha, or the people who arose around him, had to deal with this. Somehow the masters of this line seem to have found a way to keep that extraneous being out of it, out of the golden whirlwind. But then again, you can see in lots of sacred Buddhist art a kind of circle of saints, painted in the air around the main saint being depicted. And these saints are connected by lines, a kind of whitish thread, to the head of the saint in center. These lines aren't abstractions, they're actually depictions of real connection. And these saints are using these lines to communicate; the main saint hears these surrounding beings in his head. I'm not sure how much better this situation is than the other."*

And he went quiet yet again. And stayed that way for a while.
So I asked him:

M: "Who are you?"

He looked up.

Q: *"What?"*

M: "Who are you?"

Q: *"I don't understand the question."*

M: "What?"

He smiled.

Q: *"Exactly. I don't understand the question. I never have. Maybe that's why I don't think properly."*

M: "What?"

Q *(laughing now): "That's right. I don't understand the question 'Who?' I know that it's a subcategory of What Questions but I don't understand it. It never made sense to me. I don't know who I am, and I don't need to know because I know what I am."*

M: "Ok. What are you?"

Q: *"I am that which says I in me."*

19

CLEANING UP

In late November of that year I realized that there was one more thing I had to do before I disappeared. I couldn't shake the feeling that there was still something going on with the larger group, that they were still looking for me actively, even when they had no reason to. I had stopped fighting with them through the dreamtime months before. I believed, though, that since they might be looking, or helping those other core few look, that it was opening doors to possession and influence on those around me that were putting everyone in danger.

The group's policy was that a potential member had to attend three meetings at one of the houses. During the meetings both the group and the potential member would evaluate what was happening, and then both would decide if the candidate could join the group. I felt I had to go back to those people and have two more meetings with them to finish the process and close the door.

Maybe the people who attacked me from the original group would be there. If they were, then my intention was confrontation, and we'd finish it right then and there. But if those people had moved on, then the meetings with the group would finish the process I'd started by going to see them the first time. As long as I didn't go back and finish the series of meetings there would always be a door open to them — a door for them to get to me through.

I hitchhiked back to St. Louis. My intention was to go to my Union Hall and register to work. When the registration was old enough for me to ship out around Christmas I would go and work one more time until the river froze so that I could get enough money to disappear with.

I got there and checked into the hotel, different room this time, and took a cab right up to their house and knocked on their door. None of the people who'd been there for that first meeting lived there anymore. Everybody in the group rotated from house to house in one city after the other, I'd been told. But I did recognize one guy. The guy who opened the door was the same guy who had been leaving for another house in another city on the evening I'd first shown up there. He had been transferred back to this house.

He recognized me, seemed happy to see me and said, "Oh hey, hi, I remember you." And I said, "Hi. I'm here to finish up those three meetings. I've got two to go." He said, "That's fine, that's fine, come on in and we'll just put your name down here in the appointment book."

We went down the hallway to a pedestal where the book was kept. He picked up a pencil and bent over, poised to write my name in the open book. I told him my name and he froze. The color drained from him. Without moving his hand or standing up, he turned his face to me with his eyes wide with fear and questioning. I stared at him and his hand started shaking. He dropped the pencil. As cold as I could I said, "That's right, put it down. Write it down and I'll be back." And he wrote it down.

So I met with them on two consecutive nights. The people in this group had a different set of physical archetypes than the ones in the first group except for one, the group leader. His structures were only partially congruent with parts of A and parts of the man who had attacked me at the first meeting with the group; but it was enough to let me know that I was communicating with a similar awareness.

They were on their best behavior; polite, smiling, and gracious. It was clear from the way they looked at me that they all knew something about what had happened the previous summer, though of course I didn't know what they knew. We met around in the dining room, the group leader and I sitting at opposite ends. I insisted that everybody keep their hands on the table. I told them to keep their hands where I could see them. They did.

The first night they showed me something about their cosmology and the second night they showed me something about their interpretation of the Tarot and how it related to the deck of playing cards. I sat there rigidly, suspicious, resisting my automatic reaction to smile back when someone smiled at me. It occurred to me that they were trying to put me at ease by being nice. Smiling back, relaxing, would have put me at an ease that I couldn't afford. And they were good at it, I even smiled back a couple times.

At the beginning of the second meeting they had asked me why I was there. I told them enough of the truth—that I was there to finish the process of three meetings. Until I did it would always feel like unfinished business. The subjects they talked about were all standard fare, the stuff they usually talked about with potential members.

The whole time though there was a clear sense that all the rest of the conversation, the exchanges that weren't just about stock material, occurred at a level of doubled meaning; everything had that extra level of meaning where we were inferring that we all knew a lot about what we were really talking about, but we were not talking about it directly, only pointing at it. At the end of it, that third meeting, I stood up and I said, "So, this ends it then, right?" The leader nodded and said, "Yes, this ends it." And he smiled at me, to show me, it seemed, that we were also ending the unspoken-of connections and events peacefully.

But it only ended it in certain ways. It didn't end for the whole group or for all the people in it.

Somewhere in there, back during all the craziness, the Chorus had told me that B's wife had died. I had gotten images of a car accident and a fire, images of a fire. And I'd been shown images of B hurt, and using a cane. I had a clear sense that he was still out there and still looking for me. I had a clear sense that A was still driving him on. And some images of other people, too. Maybe looking for revenge, I don't know. But still looking for something, anyway. Looking for me.

The dialogue years later:

M: "Why hands where you could see them? That seems a little extreme to me. These weren't the kind of people who used guns."

Q: *"Really? You don't think murder and abduction are extreme? Maybe they'd have used guns, maybe not. I was tempted to. But the hands thing wasn't about guns. It was about making signs. There are certain arts where making signs with the hands have impacts. I didn't want any sign-making under the table."*

M: "So what happened to them? The group, I mean."

Q: *"The group went on for a couple years. Then the public profile, leaving bookmarks in books in stores, stopped. The phone numbers for the different houses in different cities went disconnected. They had other properties, too. Farms and businesses, I don't know what happened to them. I didn't look too hard.*

You should know, though, I had thought almost from the beginning that I was dealing with a group within the group. Some part of the group, operating under A's control, with B and others like him, collecting energy and transferring it to her."

M: "What? You can collect energy? Transfer it? What is it, like stamps or coins?"

Q: *"No, not like stamps or money. Remember what I said about stealing energy? Energy is substance in motion, and it takes forms. Tune to the vibratory rate of the substance, or tune to the rate and pattern of the motion, or tune to the shape of the form, and when you match these, when they resonate, energy can be transferred. Portals can be opened, and people can be tracked, even after death. Energy can move from one place to the next; physical energy, emotional energy, mental energy, and even energies higher than that. I had proof of that in the first meeting with these people.*

Energy can be taken, and used by those who develop the power to take it; used for their own purposes."

M: "Used for what?"

Q: "Food. It can be used as food, either to be consumed directly, and spent on magical tasks, or used to build what are called 'higher bodies', just like regular food is used to build and maintain the physical body."

M: "Why? I mean, why would anybody do that?"

Q: "Because it's easier than doing the work necessary to create those substances on one's own. Doing it oneself is hard work, and may require help and support and assistance. In some of my studies I've even encountered the idea that it may be almost impossible to do it oneself in the conditions of modern life. Something to do with the way we use electricity, and the shortness of our lifespans.

There's apparently a whole science to it, an almost unknown science, of which things like alchemy and qi gong are traces and remnants. Or maybe these are actually the beginnings of a true science of human nature and possibility. Although, I should say, this power of taking energy is shadow alchemy. There are descriptions of paths where one can do this work on one's own, or with another person. Tantra, as it's properly understood, is an example of a path, called a left hand, or red path, of dual cultivation. Tantra is generative; it creates and changes energies without having to take something from somebody that isn't yours.

You should know also that I've found evidence that there is a long standing practice in certain monastic traditions in the East. When a newcomer is initiated, a connection to the master or guru is established and a portal is opened, so that any energy created by the initiated as they go through their daily exercises can be sent to the guru to be used by him to complete his own higher bodies. I've even heard of one modern order where the initiates deliberately volunteer to serve as food for their guru for this purpose. It brings them bliss. I've seen one of the sacred paintings of this group: it shows a long line of people several wide walking up to and through a hole in their guru's belly where the second chakra would be. The belly is shown transparently, and is filled with people inside.

The rationale is that the initiate is usually seeking higher states of consciousness, ecstatic states of consciousness, and is content with those, and isn't using the substances for higher completion. At this level, devotees sometimes do it voluntarily out of what they call Love. Later, if a student shows promise, this would change.

And in this way, by completing higher bodies, the guru is able to make choices after death about things like reincarnation.

At least that's the story. It's not widely known, but it is discoverable with a little research."

M: "So you thought that was why they were looking for you?"

Q: "Yes, to turn me into food, basically. Or if not that, then with me dead, there would be no one to oppose them and their plan to use the seekers in their groups as energy sources.

When I disappeared, I disappeared mainly to hide from them. Oh, I had other reasons too, like the Waiting, and the fact that it was completely unsafe for me to be around other people, both for them and for myself.

The more distance I had from people the less entangled I was in their thoughts and feelings, and the less crazy I appeared to them. I was always afraid of another breakdown in public, and getting arrested again, and then institutionalized.

But mostly it was to hide from those people in the Group. They'd killed a man. They could take possession of people. They had tried to kidnap me off the street.

What else could I do? Go to the cops? And tell them what? That I was in danger from a bunch of evil crazy people with magic powers?

So I went off-grid. No interaction with any government agencies. No identification.

Oh, they still targeted me psychically, but since they physically couldn't find me, they were off target a lot. Those connections require renewal and recharging, or they fade with time and distance, unless they crystallize. Destroying a crystallization takes a lot of work, running and disappearing were a lot easier. Eventually, I think they just ran out of energy for it.

They did set traps in the collective unconscious, in the dream sphere. Everybody leaves traces there. But I was up against so many other things all the time that my paranoia about them faded as the years went by. There are lots of things out there to make life dangerous for a dreamer.

I remember one day out in the wilderness, sitting on my porch all day with my rifle, waiting for them to come, because I'd had a dream the night before that had the qualities of prescience about it. I'd dreamed that they had found me and come for me. What made the difference was that in the dream I hadn't remembered the dream, and was unprepared when they showed up. But in this timeline, I remembered, and sat there, armed and waiting, and they didn't come. Maybe sometimes that's all it takes to change things for the better: remember what you would otherwise forget.

Eventually circumstances forced me out of the wilderness. I lost my residence; there was no work for me. Maybe they found some people around me, the people I depended on for livelihood, and turned them. Maybe what little good luck I had ran out. It felt like something that had been supporting me was withdrawn and I was reduced to following the Way from place to place. It was very bad for me, very painful. At least, I am still alive.

Now, a lot of them are dead of old age. Some of them seem to have long since refocused their lives elsewhere. A few years ago I stopped looking in my rearview mirror to see if I was being followed.

And you remember what one of the triggers was for me telling you the story the first time, right?"

M: "Yeah, I do. You told me that you'd sent out an inquiry to see if you were still being sought, and you'd heard a voice telling you 'We know where you are.'"

Q: "Yeah, I heard B's voice coming through one of those higher audio chakras. Well, in these past five years, it turned out to not be quite as immediately dangerous as I was afraid it was. I was contemplating disappearing again after I told you the story the first time."

M: "Why didn't you?"

Q: "By everything I can tell, I wasn't found by the living. It seems I was found by the dead. And there's not much running from that."

M: "Did you ever answer the last question, the one about the proper way of being?"

Q: "Perhaps. Not yet to my satisfaction. "

M: "Do you have any idea?"

Q: "I'm thinking. About what I want to say and whether or not to tell you.

I'll give you a partial answer. You have to have a Conscience. Having a Conscience is maybe the most painful thing there is. Fortunately, or not, most people don't have one. They have their beliefs instead.

And a Conscience is something that has to be built. It has to be developed. The underlying neurological structures are there, or rather mostly there, but they have to be connected up, and they're barely used. Maybe I'll write a book about it.

Try this one: Become Being Good."

20

WAITING

So after the last meeting with the group I left St. Louis and hitch-hiked back to the mountains. After I got back I stopped by a little grill and deli at the school. They had good sandwiches and a view of the mountains, and the cook liked me because I left good tips. I was sitting there and wondering, feeling at loose ends, and I just sort of posed this question to the universe, "What should I do next?"

And up popped that Being, the one with whom I'd struggled, and who had told me not to look upon its face.

A vision just opened in the space before me and there was that Being in the middle of it, not making any attempt to conceal himself now that I knew what he looked like, and he said, "Wait." and the vision closed up and disappeared.

(Heavy sigh)

I want to think about what I want to say next.

(And the recorder clicks off. After a silence he turned it on again.)

That's pretty much it. That's why I've been waiting for almost forty years. That's why I've been in hiding all these years. This is why, all these years, whenever you asked me what I was doing I would say 'waiting'. You asked me to tell you the story and you've been my friend for ten years, waiting for me waiting, and I think I know you well enough to trust you; to trust what kind of man you are.

School was no longer a possibility, of course. So I went and worked on the River that winter until the River froze up. There's a bend in the River between Cairo and Cape Girardeau. Coming upstream the River turns, and then you're heading south against the River flowing north. Then there's a second bend when it turns 180 again and then you cut back, heading north again with the River flowing south. Some folks call it Dogtooth Bend.

All the early winter ice flows down into that bend, and builds up there. I had always worked the boats until The River froze, and that meant that a lot of the time I was on the last boat in, the last boat through the Bend. That year there were three boats with tows stuck south of the bend, and the ice was so thick none of us could get through.

It would have cost too much to tie up the boats in a town that wasn't their home port, so the orders came down to bring the boats upriver. Break the ice, bring the boats, but leave the tows behind. Each of us was supposed to try to break through, one at a time, then the others could follow. Twelve hours our boat tried, pounding and beating against the ice, gathering speed, sledding up over it, and our weight breaking it down, flow pushing it back to the props to be ground up into cubic foot chunks or so. The deck shook so hard you couldn't hardly keep coffee in a cup.

We didn't make it. One of the other boats had tried before we got there; it had two thirds our horsepower and had failed. The third boat had half our horse, and didn't even bother to try. So the Captains conferenced.

You remember how big those motors were? We weren't diesel generator run electric motors, like locomotives. We were diesel run motors as big as locomotives themselves; in-line sixes and eights and twelves with pistons as big across as your shoulders, pounding into the cranks, rockers rattling like madmen shaking skillets filled with stones.

The Captains decided to give it one last try together. Each boat pulled an empty out of its tow and faced up to it. Then the deckhands lashed the barges together, and then we lashed the boats together, all with one inch braided steel cable drawn round the capstans.

And so, three abreast, with the barges leading like extended bows protecting the boats we roared into Dogtooth Bend. All watches were up for this. Pilots watched their Captains and the Captains watched each other.

Rudder controls in parallel, across all three boats, making the curves, staying within the buoys, sliding sideways like fishtailing in a snowy parking lot. Synching the tachometers, synching the rpm's on the screws so we started to vibrate in resonance—the screws vibrated at the same frequencies, just off the tach set readings, a fine tuning, and when we hit resonance there was a surge of power, and a sense of ease and order falling over chaos as the shaking of the boats synched, and we surged forward, three as one.

Huge, twenty feet high and forty foot long rooster tails of ice chunks flew up in the air aft of the stern. Mist froze into ice on the tow knees; the decks required safety lines just to cross. A deckhand got his boots frozen to the steel up on the empty knee deck. We pounded ahead just like it was still steam.

A generator, big as a bulldozer engine, blew out on the smallest boat. Lost their hydraulic pressure, running the back-up pumps, the Captain sweating, veins bulging as he struggled to keep the rudder sticks in play, forward, always forward, never cut the wake, you'll brake and stall. Quick, we swung an electric line across, pulled it up and pushed it across, so they could hook it in to their panel while they struggled to bring their main generator back online. When they brought it up, matching the phase shifts almost blew our generator too.

We made it, and made it proud of Union power.

We broke up with the other boats. Then we tied up for the winter, and I stepped ashore for the last time on my birthday. And then I disappeared into the wilderness for five years.

I started to do a lot of studying, a lot of reading and research, trying to figure out what had happened. I knew that things like this had had to have happened to other people before me. And I hadn't understood any of what was happening to me while it was happening.

While I was telling you this story I was trying to keep it real, just tell you the data of what happened and keep that clear, not mixing it up with a lot of interpretation and the things I discovered later. At the moment, I'm unwilling to share what I've learned about what happened and the significance of what happened. Some of what I learned is legendary and it's not recorded anywhere; it comes from the stories and beliefs of other people that I've heard in conversation and in passing.

Often people would say these things to me almost at random, sometimes completely out of context, and it's been really unclear why they were talking about these things when I was around. Other things that I've learned are things that I've seen in obscure books, and seen referenced in other books. Many of these books are no longer in my possession. Some of these are references that I can no longer find or no longer recall the source.

Many of these things I learned I shall keep to myself, maybe to tell you at a later time, maybe never to tell. Others may recognize what these things mean if they hear this tale, and if they do, then blessings on them. It's never done me much good thinking about those things and right now I can't imagine that talking about them would bring either of us anything other than grief.

That is not an idle imagining either. I've had to pay, and pay a lot, for everything I've ever done that wasn't waiting. Even working to get food to eat so that I could survive again to wait another day. What do I mean by pay for? I mean I've had to suffer in extraordinary ways sometimes in order to obtain the most simple and necessary things. And for much of my life, most of the work I could get was simple forms of manual labor.

I was so afraid. I was afraid of doing anything, because anything I did might be a violation of the waiting. And if I violated the waiting then maybe the deal I made that required that the price of mankind's freedom was my freedom might be off, and I couldn't stand the thought of it.

What I mean is, I didn't know whether or not the part of the deal where the price was my freedom meant just the one time, or for my entire life. If it required my freedom for my entire life, then being told to wait was part of the deal. And I couldn't take the chance that it was otherwise. So everything that wasn't waiting had to be paid for, so that it didn't change the deal.

It was a very clever trap. And self-defeating, the most twisting of traps, this being had put me in. That's how it felt. Reason could only go so far in figuring out what it might mean with so little data. A thing is either one thing, or it isn't; it's a separate thing. But what if it's both? How does Reason find the way to do and not do, both at the same time? I could neither do nor not do.

I remember a series of days where nothing happened for the entire day that I did not dream about the night before. Every gesture, every word, all dreamed about before I did them. And where was freedom in that?

There is no freedom if everything happened as it was dreamed it would, as prophesied it would happen, so to speak. Even my own nature and being were telling me that freedom was impossible, hopeless, and fruitless. I was driven to despair.

And one day I hit upon an idea. If I did nothing, just did nothing, and kept on doing nothing long enough, that there would have been nothing to dream about, and therefore, maybe no dream of doing nothing. So I toyed with the idea in my mind. And of course I dreamed about toying with it, too.

After about three days of this I suddenly decided to do it. I was sitting down, leaning on a table, and I just stopped doing anything. No movement, no active thought, just watching my dreaming of doing what I was doing, which was nothing at all, washing through my mind, running like a double image on the screen of what I was looking at in the room.

This lasted for a few hours. Even the light changing as the sunlight moved across the room was as I had dreamed it. And then my memory of the dream showed that the dream was coming to a kind of fork in the road. If I just continued to do nothing a little while longer the part of my mind that was dreaming the future uncontrollably would get, would have gotten, bored and switched to another prescient dream about some other time further in the future.

And it happened. The dreamer went off and dreamed another dream. And I was free to do what I hadn't dreamed. So I got up and went outside and stared at the sky awhile, wondering about what kind of freedom this was.

If there were ever to be another story about those times after this story I just told you I might call it "On the Run, Abandoned by God" or "Alone in the Wilderness". The despair and the suffering and the pain of those times, when I think of them, brings a darkness over my soul and my vision of remembering. So I don't go there often.

The Being never returned again and no help ever came.

The Whirlwind showing up a second time in the Memphis jail was help, certainly. But why tell me to wait and never come back? Why bother saving my life? I do not know.

To be completely honest, something appeared to me in the wilderness one night that might have meant that help almost came. I didn't recognize the being in the moment but judging by the items it carried, a book and a scroll, research showed me that by many traditions it was archangelic help.

It appeared in gray-tone against a normal background, surrounded by a mandorla, a shape like the intersection of circles in the vesica piscis.

It appeared to me in the night, while I was sleeping. As I began to wake up to it, I was shocked to realize that it was completely self-willed, and not under my control at all. I thought it was there to attack. My response to its sudden appearance, after years of waiting, and having no clue what it was, was one of terror and rage and I became very aggressive about defending myself. It seemed shocked, and then, if possible, frightened. And then, perhaps, he seemed offended at my response. Then the mandorla collapsed and it popped out of sight.

It never came back. Other than possibly that one visitation, no one ever came. No one ever came back.

The dialogue years later:

M: "So now you're talking to me about all those things you wouldn't talk about before; all the interpretive stuff, not just the data. Why?"

Q: *"Well, because there is waiting in silence. It's been a habit of mine for a long time. I'm sure you can figure out why. There are ways in which I'm still waiting.*

But also because five, almost six, years have passed since I first told you the story. The world has changed enough, and now it's time."

M: "What's changed?"

Q stared at me silently until I realized he wouldn't answer.

M: "So everything became affected by waiting?"

Q: *"Yes. Everything. Look. Look at it consciously. There were no rules. There were no clarifying instructions about what I was allowed to do and what I wasn't. The baseline was that doing anything at all wasn't waiting. So, what could I do? It was crazy-making in the extreme. I couldn't even work on answering the question about the proper way of being."*

M: "What happened to the Path of the Heart?"

Q: "I had to give it up. Well, actually, I sacrificed it. I tried to keep it going for a while, holding it in abeyance while I waited. But even the act of holding it turned out to be a violation of the Waiting. So I let it go.

But I traded it for something; I traded it to stop a war. What I did wasn't the only thing that stopped it, but it helped. It kept our country out of a specific place until now. And we're still not there yet, either.

When I gave it up, it was taken from me like when I gave up the power of the Golden Whirlwind the first time. It left a big hole in my chest that took a long time to fill in. I had to use the higher chakras to make ethical decisions and the lower ones to make motivational decisions. Until I repaired it, my soul was open to the elements. My spirit would want to collapse with every temblor.

But I discovered something. The Heart is the roof of the Soul, and the foundation of the Spirit.

You have to understand that what I just told you is the Truth. Not about my suffering, which was true enough, but about what the Heart is. Do you? Do you understand?"

M: "No."

Q: "Look, I'll try to make this simple. Everything that wasn't waiting had to be paid for. And everything was anything that wasn't waiting. For a long time I tried to do the absolute minimum, eating, drinking water, defecating, sitting around. I would wait before I would do any of these, even.

But of course I couldn't sit, as in sit and meditate, or circulate the energies. That was doing something. Anything that resembled the path of the Crown, for example, was also out of the question.

I had to pay psychically for doing the research into what had happened to me. I had to pay extra for even finding a job to buy food to feed myself. And that's meant years of dealing with lying bosses and manual labor wages.

It seemed like the only way to continue to live without extra suffering was to not do anything, to wait until I died. I could think of nothing else that would fulfill the command to wait.

But then if I died, died the dead death, then I wouldn't be waiting anymore, would I? Even dying the dead death was out of the question.

And I have, you know. Died, that is. Several times. Fortunately there were times when I was able to get my pants down before I died. A couple times I hadn't eaten enough recently to worry about defecating. Once, I died standing up. I just refused to fall down. I had pulled up to a bad situation and was getting out of my truck when I felt the dying coming on. I pulled out my penis so I wouldn't soil myself, hung on to the open door with one hand and the steering wheel with the other, and one foot on the ground and the other on the running board, locked my legs and died. When I came back up to the light of day I shook myself off, put my pants back together and went on with dealing with the crisis in front of me. I'd died enough times by then to know the routine.

Oddly enough I discovered that by dying I was able to buy time. Long stretches of weeks when I wouldn't have to pay anything extra for doing whatever it was I had to do. I also found out that by volunteering, as it were, for even more suffering, extra extra suffering, I could buy time too.

I had to pay for talking to you the first time. It cost five years of insomnia, grief, and anger.

All this, and much more, as a consequence of choosing the path with Heart, and then sacrificing it on an altar of Life over Death. When I recovered, my Heart, no longer a path, became a factor in moderating my desires, and in generating transcendent emotions and feelings. This is what I mean by 'roof of the Soul'. These in turn served as the basis of decisions and choices I made, as the basis for indications of what was right or wrong, and maybe what was good, or not good. This is what I mean by 'foundation of the Spirit'. Every feeling and every thought was informed by the Heart.

If my Heart didn't keep me waiting, then my fear of consequences did.

So things have changed over the years as staying alive required that I be more involved with life. But through it all, the one thing I have had to wait on the most, and the most consistently, was the conscious development of self-discipline, particularly those disciplines of self-development that are part of the path of the Crown.

Sitting meditation, circulation of the energies, all these have been particularly, what's the word...I don't know. All these have been the most difficult to begin, and once begun, impossible to maintain.

A couple years ago I tried to take up sitting again. Twice a day, twenty minutes a session. On the third day I was attacked by an assassin. In vision, that is, but it probably could have hurt me badly anyway. And by then the outside world had already begun to bend toward weird, too. Legendary bird-beasts showing up in the trees outside the windows at night, cawing and crying, with a call that sounded like a scream, scaring the neighbor's children, making the old women talk. That makes it hard to empty the mind, and let those vibratory energies circulate.

Sometimes, over the years, forced out into mundane life, refraining from self-development was the only thing I could point to where I could claim to be still waiting."

M: "Why do you think the being never came back?"

Q: "Well, by waiting I was certainly kept out of the game. If you're not playing you can't fuck it up. As far as my soul is concerned, it's the same situation as the one that created the thousands of souls of the martyred dead. The same hopelessness and despair, but there's only one of me. And although sometimes I've tried to change something by prayer, or by some action at the right place and the right time, I'm not seeking vengeance, although I've spent a lot of time angry at him. I blame him for a lot of the current state of affairs that people find themselves in.

I have to say that not coming back seems to be a part of his nature. Or rather, not coming back in accordance with our expectations as humans. He'll show up from time to time, in some place that's unpredictable and do something that causes trouble. Not coming back to follow up, not coming back to fix the problems he created is what he does. Not coming back is in his nature.

And people make up all kinds of stories to rationalize that behavior, calling it 'grace' when he shows up. But that's not what Grace is. Grace is an experience that someone can have that comes from a different source, an experience that comes when the soul and the spirit have prepared and acted in a certain way.

He saved my life, told me to wait, and then never came back. For a while I thought maybe I might even owe him for coming the second time. Almost forty years I've thought about this. It was heart breaking, absolutely fucking heart breaking, that he never came back. And then I figured out that there was nothing I could do to be worthy of his return.

And that's because not coming back is in his nature. It's what he does. You have to understand that. It's his standard behavior — that's his predictable pattern.

What's that remind you of? And do you see the impact of that pattern in the suffering of the people?"

M: "There's lots of stories, even archetypal stories, that end with 'never comes back'. And a lot of people do the same thing."

Q: "Yes, and what is the impact on those not returned to? What is their suffering, and how does it make them behave?"

M: "I think I can see some of it. It can make them believe in something that's not true, and invest a lifetime of hope and faith. It can make them do things to try to make him return, to be worthy. It can break their hearts. It can make them behave the same way to others. There's more, I know."

Q: "Yes. Sons and lovers who never come back from war. Fathers who walk out and never return to their families. Mothers lost in childbirth. All these, never come back."

He watched me, silently, waiting. I went silent, too, for a second, and then I said,

M: "You know, maybe, ultimately, it's a story about Death, death being about that moment when everybody never comes back. Maybe that's why stories about the dead coming back have such power over our imaginations. Reincarnation, resurrection, Judgment Days, the Afterlife, zombies, even vampires, are all about the return of the dead."

Q: "Yes, our longing and grief over our losing of others, and our fear of losing ourselves, drives the mind into the realm of phantoms and fantasies. Very few realistically deal with the inevitable. They live unprepared for it and so often seem surprised.

But I want you to think about something else. It's not as if he's dead—he's out there. He's alive and undealt with. If he behaves this way, never coming back except to make more trouble, he must derive some benefit from it, or otherwise he wouldn't do it; a benefit derived at the expense of the suffering of the people. Just the possibility that this was true torqued up my anger. And what benefit do you think that might be?"

M: "I don't know. I can see a place for a reason in my mind, but I don't see the reason yet."

Q: "I'll let you think on it then. So as to why I think he never came back? I think he came back in the Memphis jail because he was curious. No one had ever given back the gift of the Golden Whirlwind before, and he didn't understand why. When he showed up and put his hand on me I think he was probably bored with my suffering, and wanted to make sure I never became a problem, without having to kill me. He may have even thought I might become useful to him later on. When he told me to wait I think it was because he wanted to stop me from continuing to change things. If I couldn't make something better, or more useful, I would at least try to change the outcome just on principle alone. And maybe he told me to wait as a little bit of revenge for my figuring out how to look upon his face.

And then maybe it's because we didn't really have anything good to say to each other. As I came to understand more about who he was, and what he's done to the people I came more and more to rage and rail and wail against the sky, sending all my outrage and grief at him. As I came to understand his impact on history he looked more and more to me to be some kind of outlaw raiding the settlements, and escaping back into some untrackable wilderness before a defense could be organized.

After several years it got to the point where I lost the ability to find gratitude for anything in my life. After a few months of this I realized that there was something fundamentally wrong with being in that condition. So I decided to go outside every day and stand there and force myself to experience gratitude as a feeling, even when I didn't feel it naturally. Then, by this act of remembrance, I began to recover the reasons to feel gratitude for my life, and from this flowed the feelings.

It took me a long time, until these last few years, to stop experiencing so much of my suffering as if I was the victim in all this, and as if I was his victim. It took me a long time to accept responsibility at the emotional level for it, and to recognize it as a result of choices I had made, rather than just blame it all on him.

Oh, there's still accountability and responsibility on his part; and I say that not as if there were any actual chance of being able to see it acknowledged. But accepting that there's really no chance at all, I have to tell you that there are a lot of ways in which I, too, have become bored with my own suffering."

He smiled and looked up to the right for moment.

Q: "You know, what the hell, you know? One time when I was a teenager and all full of myself I got in an argument with my folks and the upshot was that they wouldn't let me go someplace I wanted to go. And then they left.

So I got pissed and went downstairs to the basement bathroom and slammed the door and started beating on the walls with my fists, saying, 'Goddamn, goddamn fucking damn.'

But they hadn't really left quite just yet and I was yelling so loud pounding on the walls that my father heard me. So he came running back into the house and ran down the stairs and burst through the bathroom door with his fist raised ready to pop me one. And I raised my fend-off hand and pulled back with my hitter and he paused. He paused. And his face twisted up and he said 'Son, you think you're so special. But let me tell you, you're not special at all. The only reason you exist is because of a broken condom.'

And I got a stunned expression of relief on my face, and dropped my hands, and he dropped his hands and went away.

Now, a couple of times I've told that story people give me this stupid 'Oh, poor you' reaction. Bullshit. I was relieved. It meant that I wasn't born to a destiny.

It means I was an accident waiting to happen. And that's the only thing that ever made a lot of sense to me."

Q smiled again and went silent. I waited. After a while I asked:

M: "What are you doing?"

Q: *"I'm waiting."*

21

CONCLUSIONS

Most of the conclusions that I've come to, and the things I need for resolution, require that I remember that most of what happened to me is the result of other people's stories; stories that I somehow became caught up in and entangled in as some sort of *dramatis personae.* If for no other reason than that it was some combination of my physical appearance and being in the wrong place at the wrong time. Nothing I ever really would have wanted. So far, at least. All I did, at least in the beginning, was ask a question, and then try to answer it.

The overlapping resemblances of images giving rise to the automatism of associative meaning were intriguing for a little while. But since the goal was to overcome the automatism, and things mean what they mean, my fascination was ephemeral. I wouldn't want to confuse myself with any of their destinies or their stories. Identification with the forces of these destinies would have been deterministic—my choices would have become driven by them, rather than by some ideal or my own will.

Indeterminacy is the foundation upon which life is built by the universe. This is something that I knew then and now I can articulate it. And life is therefore in and of itself best lived as an expression of that Indeterminacy. That's why I made the deal for Freedom, rather than something else.

Why would you choose—why would anyone choose—to become the slave to a destiny? Even a great one? Look at how much blood and suffering great destinies have caused. Why be a slave to a destiny when you can sacrifice that slavery on the altar of Indeterminacy?

As the Prophet of Conscience once said, "If we must suffer, then suffer more beautifully."

And the deep pain of it now for me is this: those things that I told the Chorus that I wanted? Those things are no longer possible. They didn't happen, and now it is very probable that they won't. They never will. What I wanted for myself will never happen.

I am too old. As long as I was young enough I had the chance to feed the Indeterminacy. Now I am almost too old, and my future is determined by the small amount of time left to me. I am approaching over-determinacy. And you know that over-determinacy is the companion of Death.

As I approach this point, whatever leverage my survival exercised upon Indeterminacy is diminishing. And this means that my power as a signatory, as it were, to the deal may be diminishing too.

It is this line of reasoning, coupled with the certainty that I have been found by my enemies, which has led to the decision to tell this story for the first time in almost forty years, and to tell it to you.

I have no faith in It; that Being, or in Them, those that go with Him. They have shown nothing to me that would lead me to have Faith that They would keep Their part of the bargain after I am gone.

So your freedom, the Indeterminacy of your life, may lay in you knowing this story, and acting to hold them accountable.

The older I get the more the probability of this being true increases.

Sometimes I wonder what my own story would've been. I wonder what life of my own I could have had.

My life, your life, everybody's life—nobody's life will ever happen again.

The dialogue years later:

Q: *"I like the title you picked for this Chapter."*

M: "Yeah?"

Q: *"Yeah. Because maybe I've got a lot of 'conclusions' now, when I resisted making them before, and this is a very kind and clever invitation from you to get it all out."*

M: "Thank you."

Q: *"So let me think on it for a minute."*

M: "OK."

A minute turned into five, then ten. I got up, made coffee, did the dishes. About an hour later I sat down again and Q spoke.

Q: *"You know, forty years of waiting gives you a lot of time to think. So I've thought a lot about that deal, and how it cost me my freedom, and how little I've done with my life that I would have liked to have done.*

And I realized that the Freedom wasn't just Freedom from something, freedom from the destiny that had been planned for us. It was also Freedom for something. It is Freedom for possibility to flourish, Freedom for Indeterminacy.

Freedom that the many billions who have been born and died in all these years might have had a choice, some small possibility for a different destiny; might be a little less fated, a little less limited by the circumstances of their birth.

Sometimes I think of all the suffering these chances became. I can see into the suffering of others far away with this kind of seared vision that appears in my mind, kind of like the ancient definition of telepathy, and it took me a while to figure out in myself whether or not I was responsible for that suffering. Tortured myself for a long time with that one, I did.

And then I realized why I wasn't responsible for that suffering. What I was responsible for was for increasing the existence of the possibilities for that suffering. Those possibilities already exist to some extent, and what I did increased that extent. But the increase in the extent of possible suffering was matched by an increase in the extent of the possibility to have a different outcome, and to make a different choice. Even for those who were without the power to make a choice, those who could make no choice; the possibility that they could have had a choice increased, as did the chance for a different outcome.

And in the face of the chance to create such a huge change in possibility for others I have finally come to understand that the loss of my own choice, and my own chance to create the life I would have wanted is a small thing, in comparison."

M: "When you were talking about It, that Being, Them, and Him, and their part of the bargain, what were you talking about?"

Q: *"When that sign appeared in the hole in the sky it was a reassertion of the promise not to destroy the people again. In my mind, and in my prayers, and in my actions I had always thought that the original deal that was made wasn't just freedom from the outraged martyred dead, it was freedom from Them, too, and any form of that plan to destroy us all. It was not just freedom from that single plan, it was freedom from that whole destiny, by any means, that They sought to impose on the people.*

Let the people go free and let's see what we do with it.

And then sometimes I feel like even talking to you about this is 'disobeying god', even though I am neither obeying nor disobeying. It makes me afraid and sad and angry. Just thinking in terms like that puts myself within that context, in that story, when what I want to do is see the people free from the 'story' and living in the truth. But I don't feel ashamed. And that means either that I have no Conscience working, or it means that I do have a Conscience turned on and I'm doing nothing wrong. I'm doing what is right."

He paused again and sat quietly for a while, looking through the window, off into the distance. Then he took a deep breath, turned to me, and spoke:

Q: *"You know, I've always loved work. Real, physical, work. One of the best jobs I ever had, although it didn't pay worth a damn, was single-jacking. You know what that is? It's cutting a path through rock using just a hammer and a chisel. It was in a sensitive area, no dynamite, no heavy equipment allowed. Just down in the trench all day, day after day, banging away. Clear and simple.*

All this stuff, all these things we've been talking about since I told you the story, is mostly speculation. The story was real, but all this interpretation falls under the idea I told you earlier. It could be true, it might not be.

Once the supposedly impossible becomes possible, then it can become probable too. The story was real. Things I would have thought impossible became real and therefore the probability of them happening went to 100 percent. That much seems obvious to me. And I know that doesn't make much sense. But some part of me is still astonished, after all these years, that it actually happened.

And the interpretation? I have to say that maybe I've gotten a lot of it right. But I can't prove it, and I still have a high degree of uncertainty about it all. But not the majority degree.

The most certain part is that the deal, the original deal, went into effect. Standing there on the levee, talking to the sky, I could sense that those spirits of the martyred dead had never thought of the possibility of freedom from what they'd crystallized into.

And when they looked at it, and saw what it meant, there was no hesitation for them. It all went down fast, so fast even the Chorus was surprised. Too fast for anyone to stop it. And they're not coming back. It was a one shot deal.

I have an almost-image of the Chorus standing there, in ranks, eyes wide and jaws open. I have a sense they were all singing 'Aaaaaahhhhhhh'.

Beyond that I have become certain of a few things, maybe four. The first is that there is a difference between the Yahwic Immanence and the Jehovic Daimon. Do you know what the difference is? No?

In some lines of Western Mysticism the Yahwic Immanence is that name assigned to the background field of the Universe in which Creation and all its Natural Laws are embedded. All manifest reality is embedded in it; it holds all potentiality and is the burial ground of all phenomena.

On the other hand, the Daimon is an entity, a consciousness in possession of a form and reportedly has the arrogance to call itself the Creator, and with which people have historically had occasional contact and relations. The people have confused these two, much to our harm and detriment. It is out of the Immanence that observable reality was created, and not by some entity. Especially not some masculine entity.

Do you understand what I'm talking about?"

M: "No, I'm sorry, I don't."

Q: "The Immanence is somewhat like water to a fish, but way more subtle and difficult to sense. It is as Plotinus said: 'We are not separate from Spirit. We are in it.' And the Daimon, well, the poet Anne Herbert gave the world an image that points to it really well for me: 'We are bottom dwellers in the ocean of the sky, and who knows what fisherman waits for us?' Does that help?"

M: "More than I thought it would. And I don't like what I'm thinking very much."

Q: "You're right; it's not a pleasant prospect.

The second thing I am certain of is that the Way, the Great Way, the Tao, is antecedent to both the Immanence and the Daimon.

In times when there was no way out, in times when the laws of the former and the commands of the latter seemed to have me boxed in, no way out, it was only by following the Way that I got out. So long as I could remember my insignificance, remember my nothingness, remember the possibilities that exist for the people, remember Indeterminacy; I could use any of these to remember the Way, look for its indications, and follow it on out.

This tells me that the Way is more powerful than either of those first two, and that, therefore, it came before them. It runs through everything, even them.

The Way shows up here too, on the level of daily life. It is there to be discerned, and there to be followed, leading not to overdeterminacy, not to death, but to more life, and life more fully.

And sometimes the Way is to wait."

He went silent and I waited, for a while.

M: "And what's the third thing?"

He sighed.

Q: "I'm afraid the world, especially the spiritual world of human beings, is in a very difficult place, one where there's almost no way out. Maybe half the world is on the lunch menu of the Daimon in one way or another, and happy about it, too. The other half is wandering around in different dreams."

M: "Wait. Wait, wait, wait wait wait. Lunch? Are you serious?"

Q: "Wait wait. Wait, wait, wait, you say. You sound like a duck. Yes, lunch.

And it may be that your only choice is to become unpalatable.

Wait, where was I? Yes, everybody dreaming.

And waking up is difficult, and, from the point of view of the dreamer, it is undesirable. An argument could be made that this is harmless, that it offers some kind of solace in an otherwise inconsolable world.

But I'm convinced that unconsciousness in one area is an indicator of unconsciousness in another area. A person too deeply asleep won't even realize they've shit the bed, or that they're thirsty or hungry or sick. And I mean that literally and metaphorically. We become a danger to ourselves and everything living thing around us, including the Earth.

And yes, the Earth is alive. A tree shows it is alive only near and on the surface, and we say the whole tree is alive. It is the same with the planet, to put it simply. That Life is apparent on and near the surface shows that the whole planet is to be considered alive. It does not require much work to satisfy the so-called eight characteristics of life, but it does require both enlargement and shifting of the frames of reference.

Look at how people treat each other; not according to Conscience, which frankly most of them don't seem to have turned on and connected to reality, but according to moral precepts. This can be OK sometimes for a while for people who share the same beliefs, but it is really deadly for people who don't share those same precepts, and in some ways even for those who do. You only need to look at what women all over are forced to believe and accept about themselves as humans of a lesser status, and what they have to endure, in order to see this.

So let me give you an example of this dreaming. I was told once that several years ago the philosopher and ethnologist Joseph Campbell, perhaps the greatest chronicler of myth ever, when asked if he had any advice, said 'Follow your bliss.'

Well, some years passed and since this advice could be sloganized and put on a t-shirt, soon lots of people, especially the so-called New Age people, those people whom, ironically enough, thought of themselves as the hope for a new world, the bringers of a new paradigm, suddenly all seemed to have heard this advice, and went off to pursue their 'bliss'.

For some this meant going off to study eastern religions and disciplines, but you remember what I said earlier about many of those schools, right? How they used their people? Basically, as lunch.

For others it meant pursuing endless rounds of self-discovery workshops, all of which promised happiness in one form or another, but somehow only the people who ran these seemed to be happy. Other people set themselves up as New Age teachers of this and that tradition which they really had no permission to teach, but they made it their business to do so.

So to speak.

Yes, I can tell by your face you want to protest my over-broad generalizations, and reassure me that it was not all bad, that some teachers were real and good, and some people actually got something real. Yes, I know all that but that's not what I'm talking about.

I'm talking about what I'm talking about.

And the problem got so bad after several years that Joseph Campbell felt compelled to clarify himself and he pointed out that he hadn't intended that people run around seeking happiness and self-fulfillment. He said something like, 'Bliss, properly speaking, is an attribute of the enlightenment.' And that if someone understood what bliss actually and truly was, and then pursued it, that they would come closer, if not close, to what is actually the highest and most profound experience possible for humans.

All that probably won't fit on a T-shirt."

M: "But is it possible to get there any other way?"

Q: "Look. You were talking about credulity earlier on, right? People are told all kinds of shit and they believe it. You remember Roy G. Biv?"

M: "Wait a minute. You mean the mnemonic? For the colors of the rainbow?"

Q: "Yes. For decades, maybe longer, students all over the world were taught, and are probably still being taught, there were seven colors in a rainbow, seven colors in the spectrum of light. There is no such thing. There are only six colors. There is no indigo."

M: "Wait. There is no indigo?"

Q: "Yes. There is no indigo. It is a pigment, it is not a color of prismatic light. And here's my point. Millions of people believed that it was. Hell, I used to believe it was, after all, it's what I was taught. But if you look, there's no such thing. Me, and millions of others looked at it and thought we saw it there, and the only reason why is because those in positions of authority said it was so.

But it wasn't and it isn't, and it just ain't so.

And then, think of all those people who have spent their lives fantasizing that there are seven colors in the spectrum and that these colors correspond somehow to the seven chakras. And have been using this belief as a visualization in their meditations, trying to accomplish something spiritual by incorporating a falsehood.

Ridiculous, just ridiculous. It's both funny and tragic."

M: "So you're saying that there's a real effect on someone who believes something false?"

Q: "Yes, there is. Personal evolution starts as a state of consciousness and then becomes a state of being. Like any other state of awareness it also has a correspondence with a state of the body—a metabolic and sensible state. As someone works on themselves they attain those states, at first only for moments and then for longer periods of time.

As these times are extended the metabolic process changes begin. Eventually the state of consciousness can become permanent, or the ability to access the state of consciousness becomes at will, but perhaps more importantly the changes to the body become permanent, or at least continue on subliminally.

And if you incorporate falsehoods you'll get false results.

It is the same with lower states of higher consciousness too. Many of these techniques can be learned from all the so-called trainings and schools out there, many of the techniques are valid. But you have to be willing to experiment, rather than believe, and you have to make sure you stay off the menu.

The ultimate states of consciousness are beyond what is called 'non-dual awareness'. They all involve a Return to the world, an involvement with the world that must carry unitary awareness back into sensation. Which means suffering, of course, conscious suffering in the objective sense, which, from an egocentric viewpoint, who would want to do?

The work of doing that, the labor required to intentionally return with that awareness is an absolute necessity if someone wants to develop a conscience and fully experience the meaning of life. And there are moments, such exquisite moments of beauty, which surpass any non-dual awareness states of consciousness when one is withdrawn from this world. This beauty, the beauty experienced when one goes past the non-dual and Returns to this world, can't be gotten any way else, and the beauty known by those who never go is a pale and ghostly thing in comparison.

At this point, perhaps, if you're still sane and whole—which means something very specific—a person could be said to have attained enlightenment. But they must have the light, and something else as well. And, phenomenologically speaking, attaining the enlightenment is not the same as being enlightened, nor is it the same as having been enlightened."

M: "What do you mean, something else. What else?"

Q: "You must begin the activation of the Higher Heart, which is something very specific and palpable. It is not just a metaphor.

In any event, no matter how it is one comes by that level of awareness, it is almost impossible to maintain it constantly under the conditions of modern existence. Among other reasons, it is simply too painful. It can be constantly and relentlessly painful. And where is ecstasy then?"

M: "I don't know. I can barely imagine. Maybe I'm only imagining that I can imagine. I think I understand what you're saying, but then it vanishes like vapor in the breath on a cold morning. I still don't understand why you won't tell me more about the meaning of life."

Q: "Because if I tell you, it will be just words in your head. Right now, as you are, I won't even tell you how to find it, and for the same reason. What I want you to know is that there is a meaning to life, and that it can be found and that it can then be lived consciously. It, the answer, is embedded in the fabric of the universe, there to be discerned. But it is like those other questions.

You must formulate the question for yourself. And in addition to just thinking the question you must also sense the question and feel the question. All three parts are necessary. And then you must ask yourself the question of how to figure it out. And you must sense, feel and think this question also.

And then, if you make this into an essential issue for yourself and are willing to drive yourself crazy figuring it out all the while remaining sane and present to your daily life, then maybe you have a chance. And then the answers will be yours, it will belong to you. It will belong to your senses, your feelings, and your thoughts.

I assure you the answer is worth every moment of your struggle. And I assure you also, moreover, that the answer is not a relative answer, special to your ego alone. It is an absolute answer, true everywhere and always. And that, should you so choose, the answer will manifest through you in every detail of your everyday life, in every facet of your relative existence, and your life will gain in beauty and usefulness."

I started to say something, and then I paused and Q watched me, waiting. Then I focused on the last thing I remembered being clear about.

M: "So how do I avoid becoming lunch?"

He smiled.

Q: *"Ah, now you're thinking. Good. You cannot count on meeting a Returned One—someone who has been there and back, someone bringing unitary awareness back into sensation—to help you. They are very rare, and often about their own business anyway, because there is another kind of work to be done by those who can do it. And you cannot count on recognizing one if you met one. Mostly you are likely to meet an impostor, some practitioner of illusion spirituality. They practice a kind of hypnosis, even a charismatic hypnosis. It will make you feel good, especially about yourself. A terrible irony, I know, that on the way to ecstasy you will be trapped by feeling good. So, you cannot count upon feeling good as a sign that you are on the right path. You would probably be better served by looking for the opposite feeling; look for what makes you uncomfortable.*

But that's not the main thing. The main thing is that you have to elim-
inate your capacity to be hypnotized. And that includes gaining control
over your capacity for self-hypnosis and your vulnerability to the little
lies you tell yourself that make you feel good. As with bliss, truly feeling
good about yourself only happens when you deserve it. And you alone can
know that, but you have to stop lying to yourself about both yourself and
the world around you. And if you can do that you reduce the chance that
you'll believe someone else lying to you, too. If you eliminate the capacity
to hypnotize yourself and eliminate the capacity that allows you to be hyp-
notized by others, you stand a chance at staying off the menu.

Got it?"

M: "I hear the words. I know that in order to understand the words I
have to experience the meaning of them as a sensation. In addition
to that embodiment I have to also embody the desire to know, rather
than to believe. I know this takes remembering, and practice.

No hypnosis, by self or others."

Q: *"What about feeling?"*

M: "Oh, sorry. I forgot. Yes, feeling, too."

Q: *"What? Forget about feeling? Are you nuts? How many times have I*
talked to you about feelings and about how fatal it potentially is to ignore
feelings? Remember the Riddle? You have to actually go back and get your
feelings again. You only have to take your Soma with its senses and your
mind, your Spirit, with your thoughts, across the River once. But you
have to take your Soul across the River three times, and to do that the
fourth crossing is taking it back across to where you started. And then,
in the end, you have to go back and get your Soul for its third time in the
seven crossings of the River."

M: "Yes, but is there any other reason?"

Q: *"Are you kidding? Is there any other Reason? No. You must be whole."*

M: "Yes, I see. I must be whole. If not, I fail to complete my task."

Q: *"Good. That's the Meaning of the Riddle. So long as your mind is a cabbage how can any of your feelings be any different than those of a sheep? And how can the wolf of your bodily instincts be taught to behave? Any other questions at this moment?"*

M: "No. I'm just sitting with it, letting it sink into my body, tracking the sensation."

Q: "Good. Take another moment then."

He paused and looked out through the window and off into the distance. Then he asked, *"Do you know what a moment is?"*

M: "No. I do have another question, though."

Q: "Good. You told the truth. Another time, then. What's your question?"

He grinned.

M: "What is that other work, the work of the Returned Ones?"

Q: "Very good. You think you might be able to recognize them by the work they do? Yes?"

I nodded.

Q: "You probably won't be able to. They could be doing anything. The difference is in how they're doing it. Whatever it is they might be doing they are also doing something else. They are consciously doing something the world needs doing. And that, whatever it is, will be helping to maintain the possibility that you will lose the capacity for hypnosis. Because that is what the world needs you to do. They will be helping to maintain that other world, the real one, the one where you might have a chance, and a choice.

Perhaps if you could see in five or six dimensions you might recognize it."

M: "I have no idea what that means."

Q: "You might."

M: "Are you a Returned One?"

Q: *"Oh, you think you're funny, do you? Yeah, I see you laughing. Yeah, well, laugh at this: At the moment, not completely."*

M: "What?"

Q: *"Returned."*

M: "I am."

Q: *"I see. Again with the jokes. No, of course you're not. What you are, though, is present and paying attention."*

M: "Yes."

He held up his hand, palm toward me, and I felt a kind of push. It kept me from falling out of attention.

Q: *"And so. The final conclusion, for today anyway, is that this energy, this vibratory energy that has been with me ever since it was returned to me that night in jail, is a real thing. I don't know for sure what it means. The texts are unclear, which means to me that it is probably uncommon, if not deliberately obscured.*

Over the years I've tried, and had to suffer for it, approaching various so-called teachers about what it is, and they've either told me to ignore it, or shrugged it off as nothing.

What I think it may be is the heartbeat of higher bodies; it is the presence of the Higher Heart.

I know it's real because it's transmissible.

Other people can feel it. It can become active in them; it can also become inactive if attention isn't paid to it, especially in the beginning. After a while it can become permanent.

I remember…well, never mind."

M: "What? Never mind what? Don't stop now."

Q: "Why not? Everything I say to you is just words, just an abstraction that you know nothing about subjectively. What good does it do you or anybody else?"

M: "Because I want to know. I want to know what this is, what it feels like. I want to be more real than I am. I want to live life more fully. I have listened to you, and worked with you all these years, and this thing, this vibration, this resonance, is all that's left after the story is done. It's all that's left after the words are over. It's the residue of the whirlwinds. And if I can become more real, then I can become more Indeterminate. I can help Freedom to live."

Q: "Look, right now you have all the freedom that ignorance can provide. That may be even more freedom than the freedom that knowledge provides. Why screw it up?"

M: "For Beauty. And something in me tells me not to let the moment pass."

He went silent again for a while. Then he looked up, looked me right between the eyes, until I had to look away.

Q: "I can do this. But I'm not going to do it in the usual way. The usual way would be for me to put my hands on you, to bless you, as it were, on your head or on your shoulder. Or hold your hands. Then to run the energy of it down into you, filling you with it until you felt it for yourself.

But I'm not going to do that. If I did that, I'd be taking responsibility for you. And I can't do that.

If you were to fall out, maybe go crazy if the Release of the Serpent happened, I would be obligated to you, I'd have to take care of you. In the old days, the people in the monastery would care for you, and I'm just one old man.

But there is another way. I can do this so that the Earth becomes responsible for you. You will become, not my child, but a child of the Earth.

Do you understand? No, of course you don't. The Earth will care for you. Follow the Way.

So. You ready?"

I nodded.

Q: *"No, you can't just nod. You have to say so. You have to say, 'Yes.'"*

M: So I said it. "Yes."

Q: *"Then come stand behind me and put your hands on my shoulders. I will pull the power of it up through the Earth. You will feel the charge of it first, like a shock. Then it will surge up in you, and by the time it reaches your head it will begin to pulse. It will feel like a different heart than your own."*

And that's how it was. I stood behind him, and put my hands on his shoulders. I felt him synchronize his breath with mine, and then I felt a brief pulling sensation on my hands. Then a charge like a shock passed through me, from the ground up, and my feet started to pulse. The pulse rose up through me.

When it got to my shoulders, and rolled down my arms into my hands I heard him say, *"There."* Then I felt a barrier come up under my hands and I couldn't sense him there anymore.

The pulse fed back into my shoulders and up my neck and throat into my head. When it got to my eyes the field of vision started to vibrate at the edges and then slowly closed down in darkness, narrowing to a long tunnel, where the edge was like the trembling petals of some dark flower blooming inward on itself.

Then my mind filled in an instant with a golden light, a light that left me blind, and senseless, and thoughtless, and in ecstasy.

I slowly sank to my knees. Still blinded by light, I felt-sensed him standing up and stepping out of my field.

Then I heard him, just the floor creaking under his weight, but step-less, no sound of foot falls, the sound like the sound of the ghosts in the hallway at night.

I sensed him smiling as he turned at the door, opening it as he turned.

He stepped through and said, *"I'm guessing this will be a Blessing for you by the end. With this closing door between us, we are separate to fend."*

Epilogue:
THE RIVER

From the original recording:

There's one more thing I want to say, one more tale I want to add to this story. I had the chance several years later to cross the country again. I stopped and slept in my truck one night in a campground on the bluffs of the upper reaches of the Mother River. A friend of mine had come down from Minneapolis to talk to me as I was passing through.

When I woke up the next morning the mist from the river was high, rising up over the bluffs and blowing easily into the woods.

We walked the trail down to the overlook. It was autumn and the leaves had turned a hundred colors and the spiders had woven a hundred thousand webs in the woods. The mist had left droplets of water over all of these; the edges of the leaves, the countless webs. And when the rising sun shone through it the entire forest burst into a million sparkling diamonds of light.

The vision of it, and being immersed in that vision, filled us with marveling joy. My friend had his young son with him, and, holding his father's hand as they walked down the trail ahead of me, the boy simply burst into spontaneous song. He made up a lyric: 'I love life. I love the world. I love life because it's beautiful.' He sang it over and over as we went down the trail. And I walked through this sparkling sunrise in awe and gratitude for Beauty.

And then I knew, right then I came to know, that if you could just Love Life—that if you could just hang on and Love Life hard enough and long enough and well enough and wise enough—that Life would become aware of you, and that Life would Love you back. And that would bring you all the Love you needed and you'd never have to use any of your Love on loving your Self.

When I got to the overlook, I climbed down over the side. I eased myself as far down the bluff in the long grass of the overhang as I dared. I wanted to offer thanks to the Spirit of the River for saving my life. The mist was so high, as high up as I was, and swirling around me, and so thick I couldn't see the river. So I waited, leaning out, hanging on to the long grass with one hand, disappointed that I couldn't see Her. Then I sent a voice, asking for Her to come and see me.

Suddenly a column perhaps twenty-five feet across opened up in the mist, and I could see clearly straight down to the river a hundred feet below. The sun light broke through to the surface of the water, and then a form rose up and floated, stretching from one side of the column to the other, silver on the silver water.

She was there, floating on Her back, an exquisite form of naked risen silver, Her long silver-black hair swirling away in the current. She smiled at me. I dropped the offering and said, "Thank you, thank you for saving my life. Thank you." and She smiled again and sank away, swirling down river in the current, and the column of clear vision closed in swirls of silver white light.

This is what I have to say.

FROM THE AUTHOR

The novel you have just finished reading, *American Siddhi*, is the first in a series called *The Siddhi Wars*.

Siddhi is a Sanskrit word for 'accomplishment' or 'attainment' and refers to the development of magical or psychic powers.

This is not the same word as Sidhe (pronounced sheeth-uh) which refers to a supernatural race in Irish mythology.

There are many Siddhi powers. Some authorities say eight, another says five, yet another says there are more than one hundred. For our purposes, anyone with a magical or psychic power will be considered Siddhi. And someone can develop more than one power.

One of the difficulties for a Siddhi is the cultural context in which those powers arise, and the beliefs in that culture around those powers. In some cultures they are celebrated, in others they are considered evil and must be repressed. In yet other cultures, they are allowed to manifest in only certain narrow contexts, say, for example, as in a faith healer.

Siddhi powers may arise as a result of certain kinds of work on one-self. At other times it seems that the cause of a power arising can be accidental—some impact, some dramatic moment, and the power is simply there. It appears that some powers have a genetic component; they are passed from generation to generation, and may arrive with birth or reveal themselves at some other threshold. And finally, it appears that these powers can be transferred to someone, as in given as a gift, especially if the receiver is ready, but not necessarily.

Moreover, many Siddhis believe that their power arises because of the culture in which they developed, and they behave as if it is that culture to which they owe their power. Perhaps this is true, to a certain extent.

But it is also true that there are times when the causes are accidental, as accidental as where one is born. It is also possible that the development of Siddhi powers is evidence of the evolutionary potential of the human species, rather than evidence of the spiritual attainment of the individual.

Confusions about these matters, and conflicts between them, can lead Siddhis into conflicts as proxies for the conflicts between their cultures. Gone, perhaps, are the days when a poet could sing a curse that could stop an invading army. But there are smaller and more subtle displays of power all around us. Perhaps, in the near future, this will become apparent, and the conflicts then will be between those who have and those who have not on the one hand, and on the other, there will be the conflict between those who have, and are in service to the good, and those who have and are in service either to that which is not good, or are in service only to themselves.

It is not yet determined who the "winners" will be.

The second novel in the series *The Siddhi Wars* is called *Stonehaven*. Stonehaven is a working farm and a remote mountain retreat center and yoga school, much like those remote mountain retreat centers that host retreats for various contemporary schools and workshops. And Stonehaven is much more than that. Those businesses act as support for, and also a cover for, an unusual college. Stonehaven is a college for the training of Priestesses to serve in the Restoration of the Divine Feminine to Her proper place.

Please keep reading to see a selection from the novel *Stonehaven*.

SELECTION FROM:
STONEHAVEN

She closed her eyes, and still she could feel the pulse over the land, thrumming even though the drums had long since stopped. In her own heart and belly she felt it, too, and she synchronized her heart and breathing with it.

Awake now, she swung her feet around and onto the floor. She glanced at the alarm clock, and panicked again; then she remembered that it was the first day of summer, and that she was not on the early shift for breakfast. Not many would be needed then, for not many would have risen, but she was on duty for brunch, one of the only four times of the year this happened.

She slipped on her summer robe and sandals and went down the four flights of stairs to the basement and the kitchen. The crew was there, Thomas and Elizabeth and Marion. The woman she now knew as a Priestess, Diana, was there too, dressed in a deep blue silk summer robe loosely belted and hair down, leaning against a counter with her arms crossed over her chest and legs crossed at the ankles. She had been talking to the others when Angelica came in. Diana looked up at her and smiled.

Angelica could hear people moving upstairs in the dining room, and asked after David, the last member of the scheduled crew, and Diana told her that he was upstairs, finishing up with the early risers meal.

Angelica squinted her eyes in an attempt to discern Diana's mood and availability. Diana smiled at her and uncrossed her arms, so Angelica asked her, "Do you have a minute? I'd like to talk to you about a dream I had last night."

Diana said, "Sure," and nodded her head toward the shade garden, dappled now in rising morning sunlight during only these few short weeks of the year. They got cups of coffee from the urn and went outside, sitting at a garden table with chairs.

Putting her feet up on an adjacent empty chair, and arranging her robe, Diana said, "So, tell me."

Angelica hesitated, then she drew a breath and blew it out. "Do you feel it? Do you feel the pulse that's all over the land?"

Diana smiled, "Yes, in fact, I do. Do you know where it comes from?"

"Yes," Angelica said. "It comes from the Sunken Garden. It started last night during the Ceremony and radiated out from there. How'd it happen? You were there, right? What did you all do?"

Diana smiled even more broadly. "Yes, it started there, and yes, also, I was there. As for what happened there and as for you, you'll have to wait to see. Now, you said you had a dream?"

"Yes," Angelica said, "I dreamed I was at an ancient version of the Ceremony, and this is what I saw." Angelica proceeded to tell her the dream in all the detail she could recall, including the orgasm and ejaculation at the end.

Diana listened closely, smiling at some parts, shaking her head slightly at times, and watching Angelica's face intently, looking for Angelica's reactions to her dream. When Angelica had finished her tale, including waking up this morning, Diana asked her, "Do you know what that was?"

"Yes, it is one of the eight orgasms a woman can have."

"That's the anatomical answer. Do you know the ritual answer?"

"Something to do with the blessing of the rain?"

"Yes, but do you know what that means?"

"No, not really," Angelica said.

Diana said, "Well, one thing that it means is that you are going to start your studies of Tantra and Alchemy. I'll notify the Curriculum Committee, and make sure that arrangements are made."

Angelica was thoughtful for a moment, then she said, "Alright. I look forward to it." And then, after a pause, she said, "Do you think it would be OK for me to walk down to the Garden now?"

Diana said, "Alone or in company?"

Angelica said, "I think, alone."

Diana said, "Yes, you may."

Angelica took a last sip of her coffee, and stood up; then, looking to the northeast, walked to the driveway entrance to the shade garden and turned the corner. When she was out of sight, Diana stood up and slowly walked in that direction, following her.

Lightning Source UK Ltd.
Milton Keynes UK
UKHW021438151121
394002UK00011B/2745